Men and Cartoons

Men and Cartoons

Stories

Jonathan Lethem

 DOUBLEDAY

New York   London   Toronto   Sydney   Auckland

PUBLISHED BY DOUBLEDAY
a division of Random House, Inc.

DOUBLEDAY and the portrayal of an anchor with a dolphin are registered trademarks of Random House, Inc.

Versions of some of these stories first appeared elsewhere. "The Vision" (the opening paragraph of which shares several sentences with *The Fortress of Solitude,* a novel) was published in *Tin House* and reprinted in *Bestial Noise: The Tin House Fiction Reader.* "Access Fantasy" first appeared in *Starlight 2* and was reprinted in *Histories of the Future.* "The Spray" was published in *Fetish.* "Planet Big Zero" was published in *Lit* and reprinted in *The KGB Bar Reader.* "The Glasses" was published in the *Voice Literary Supplement.* "The Dystopianist, Thinking of His Rival, Is Interrupted by a Knock on the Door" was published in *Conjunctions* and reprinted in *Pushcart Prize Stories XXVIII.* "Super Goat Man" was published in *The New Yorker.* "The National Anthem" was published in *Black Clock* and was reprinted in *Lit Riffs.*

Book design by Lovedog Studio

Library of Congress Cataloging-in-Publication Data
Lethem, Jonathan.
    Men and cartoons : stories / Jonathan Lethem.—1st ed.
        p. cm.
    Contents: The vision—Access fantasy—The spray—Vivian Relf—Planet big zero—The glasses—The dystopianist, thinking of his rival, is interrupted by a knock on the door—Super goat man—The national anthem.
    I. Title.
PS3562.E8544M46 2004
813'.54—dc22

                                                            2004050039

ISBN 0-385-51216-3

PRINTED IN THE UNITED STATES OF AMERICA

December 2004

First Edition

10 9 8 7 6 5 4 3 2 1

For Thomas Berger

Contents

Men and Cartoons

The Vision

I FIRST MET THE KID KNOWN AS THE VISION at second base, during a kickball game in the P.S. 29 gymnasium, fifth grade. That's what passed for physical education in 1974: a giant rubbery ball, faded red and pebbled like a bath mat, more bowled than pitched in the direction of home plate. A better kick got the ball aloft, and a fly was nearly uncatchable—after the outfielder stepped aside, as he or she invariably did, nearly anything in the air was a home run. Everyone fell down, there'd be a kid on his ass at each base as you went past. Alternately, a mistimed kick scudded back idiotically to the pitcher, and you were thrown out at first.

The Vision booted a double. His real name was Adam Cressner, but he believed himself or anyway claimed to be the Vision: the brooding, superpowered android from Marvel Comics' *Avengers*. The comic-book Vision had the power to vary the density of his body, becoming a ghost if he wished to float through walls or doors, becoming diamond hard if he wished to stop bullets like Superman. Adam Cressner couldn't do any of this. This day he wasn't even wearing his cape or costume, but under black curls his broad face was smeared unevenly with red food dye, as it always was. I was fascinated. The Vision had come to be taken for granted at Public School 29, but I'd never seen him up close.

"Nice kick," I ventured, to Adam Cressner's back. The Vision had assumed a stance of readiness, one foot on the painted base, hands dangling between his knees Lou Brock–style. "Ultron-5 constructed me well," replied the Vision in the mournful monotone of a synthetic humanoid. Before I could speak again the ball was in the air, and Adam Cressner had scooted home to score, not pausing as he rounded third.

Now the Vision was a grown man in a sweatshirt moving an open Martini & Rossi carton-load of compact discs into the basement entrance of the next-door brownstone. I spotted Captain Beefheart, Sonny Sharrock, Eugene Chadbourne. I'd been returning from the corner bodega with a quart of milk when I recognized him instantly, even without his red face and green hood, or the yellow cape he'd worn in winter months. "Adam Cressner?" I asked. I made it a question to be polite: it was Adam Cressner.

"Do I know you?" Cressner's hair was still curly and loose, his eyes still wild blue.

"Not really. We went to school together."

"Purchase?"

"P.S. 29, fifth grade." I pointed thumbwise in the direction of Henry Street. I didn't want to say: *You were the Vision, man!* But I supposed in a way I'd just said it. "Joel Porush."

"Possibly I remember you." He said this with a weird premeditated hardness, as if not *remembering* but *possibly remembering* was a firm policy.

"Migrated back to the old neighborhood?"

Cressner placed the box at the slate lip of the basement stairwell and stepped around his gate to take my hand. "By the time we had a down payment we could barely afford this part of the city," he said. "But Roberta doesn't care that I grew up around here. She became entranced with the neighborhood reports in the City section."

"Wife?"

"Paramour."

"Ah." This left me with nothing to say except, "I should have you guys over for drinks."

The Vision lifted one Nimoy-esque eyebrow.

"When you get in and catch your breath, of course." *You and the paramour.*

I met Roberta at the border of our two backyards, the next Sunday. The rear gardens through the middle of the block were divided by rows of potted plants but no fence, allowing easy passage of cats and conversation. These communal yards were a legacy from the seventies that most new owners hadn't chosen to reverse. I had a basement renter's usual garden privileges, and was watering the plants which formed the border when Roberta Jar appeared at her back door. She introduced herself, and explained that she and Cressner had bought the house.

"Yes, I met Adam a few days ago," I said. "I know him, actually. From around here."

"Oh?"

I'd supposed he'd told of our encounter in front, mentioned being recognized by a schoolmate. Now I had to wonder whether to explain Cressner's childhood fame. "We were at grade school together, on Henry Street. Long before this was a fashionable address. Surely he's walked you past his alma mater."

"Adam doesn't reminisce," said Roberta Jar coolly and, I thought, strangely. The assertion which could have been fond or defiant had managed to be neither. I thought of how Adam had *possibly remembered*, the week before.

"Funny, I do nothing else," I said. I hoped it was a charming line. Roberta Jar didn't smile, but her eyes flashed a little encouragement.

"Does it pay well?" she asked.

"Only when something gets optioned for the movies."

"How often is that?"

"It's like the lottery," I said. "Ninety-nine percent of the time, nothing. But that one time and you're golden."

I'd been blunted from the fact of my instinctive attraction to Roberta Jar, in those first moments, by her towering height. Roberta was six two, or three, I calculated, and with none of that hunched manner with which women apologize for great height or sizable breasts. So I'd been awed before being struck. By this time, though, I was struck too. *Paramour-pyramid-pylon*, I fooled with in my head.

I mentioned again having the two of them over for a drink. My evenings were very free since parting from Gia Maucelli, and I was stuck on what I'd blurted to Adam Cressner and had visualized ever since—a grown-up encounter, involving wine and sophisticated talk. No longer a couple, I still socialized like one in my imagination. Cressner and his tall woman would visit my apartment for drinks. They'd see the couple I'd been by Gia's phantom-limb absence, and ratify the couple I'd likely be again by the fact of themselves. In other words, perhaps Roberta Jar had a friend she could set me up with.

"Maybe," she said, utterly disinterested. "Or you could come along tonight. We're having a few people in."

"A housewarming party?"

"Actually, we're playing a game. You'd like it."

"Truth-or-dare, spin-the-bottle sort of thing?"

"More interesting than that. It's called Mafia. You should come—I think we still need a fifteenth."

For bridge or a dinner party you might need a fourth or a sixth—Roberta Jar and Adam Cressner needed a fifteenth. That was how close to essential I'd been encouraged to feel myself to be.

"How do you play Mafia?"

"It's hard to explain, but not to play."

I turned up with wine, still imposing my paradigm, but it was a beer thing I'd turned up at. Adam Cressner ushered me into the parlor, which was restored—new white marble fireplace and mantel, freshly remodeled plaster-rosette ceiling, blond polished floor—but unfurnished, and full instead of gray metal folding chairs like those you'd find in a church basement. The chairs were packed with Adam and Roberta's friends, all drinking from bottles and laughing noisily, too caught up to bother with introductions—when I counted I found myself precisely fifteenth. Roberta Jar was part of the circle, tall in her chair. I wondered if she stood taller than Adam—this was the first time I'd seen them together.

Adam had just been explaining the game, and he started again for me. I was one of four or five in the group who'd never played. Others threw in comments and suggestions as Adam explained the rules. "I'll be the narrator," Adam told us. "That means I'm not playing the game, but leading you through it."

"We want you to play, Adam," someone shouted. "Someone else can narrate. We've played, we know how."

"No, you need a strong narrator," said Adam. "You're an unruly bunch." I imagined I heard in his tone a hint of the Vision's selfless patronage of humanity.

According to the rules of Mafia, the group of fourteen comprised a "village"—except that three of us were "mafia" instead: false villagers working to bring the village down. These identities were assigned by dealt cards, black for village, red for mafia. The game then unfolded in cycles of "night" and "day." Night was when we closed our eyes and lowered our heads—"The village is asleep," Adam explained—with the exception of the three mafiosi. They instead kept their eyes open, and by an exchange of glances silently conspired to select a villager to kill. The victim would be informed of his or her death by the narrator, when night was over, and then make an orderly exit from the game.

Day, by contrast, was chaos, a period of free talk and paranoia among the sincere and baffled villagers—who, of course, included three dissembling mafiosi. Each day closed with the village agreeing by democratic vote on a suspect to banish. This McCarthyesque ritual lynching brought about night, and another attack from the mafia. And so on. The mafia won if they winnowed the village down to two or three, a number they could dominate in any voting, before the village purged all mafiosi from its ranks. It seemed to me like relentless jargonish nonsense, but I worked on a beer (telling Roberta the wine was "for the cellar"), checked out the women, and allowed myself to be swept into the group's flow. We began our first day in the village, peppered by Adam-the-narrator's portentous reminders, such as "Dead, keep your silence." I'd drawn a black card: villager.

Our village was young and boisterous, full of hot, beer-bright faces whose attachments I couldn't judge. It was also splendidly bloodthirsty. "It pretty much doesn't

matter who we vote out on the first day," some veteran
player announced. "We don't have any information yet."
I wondered how we were meant to gather information at
any point in the agitated cross talk, but never mind. A
regular named Barth was quickly exiled, on grounds of
past performance—he'd proven such a generally decep-
tive player that he couldn't be trusted now. Roberta, who
with her stature and chesty volume was strongly domi-
nant in the village, led this charge. Barth succumbed to
our lynch mob under groaning protest. "Night" fell, we
"slept," and when day came again Adam announced
that a woman named Kelly had been taken out by the
mafia.

Kelly's murder drew shouts and giggles of surprise.
Why had they picked her? Perhaps *this* was the information that would lead us to an informed lynching, instead
of Barth's whimsical sacrifice. The village again plunged
into an uproar of accusations and deflection. I turned to
the woman beside me, a sylphlike girl with dyed-black
shortish hair, who hadn't spoken. "Are you in the mafia?"
I asked her, not quite whispering.

She blinked at me. "I'm a villager."

"Me too." I told her my name, and she told me hers—
Doe. Our exchange was easily covered by the shouts of the
village leadership, mainly Roberta Jar and a couple of stri-
dent men, as they led our next purge.

"First time?" Doe asked.

"Yes."

"That doesn't mean you aren't lying to me."

"No, it doesn't," I said. "But I'm not. Whom do you suspect?"

"I'm hopeless at this." Unashamed, she met my eye. I felt a pang. Doe was everything Roberta Jar was not: diminutive, vulnerable, and, I began to hope, single.

"We'll work together," I suggested. "Be watchful."

Mafia was a kind of fun, I decided. It elicited from us heaps of behavior: embarrassment and self-reproach, chummy consensus building that curdled at a moment's notice to feints of real paranoia and isolation, even measures of self-righteous, persecuted fury. The intensity was enthralling, but it was also strangely hollow, because it lacked any real content. For all the theatrics, we revealed nothing of ourselves, told no tales. It was that for which I yearned.

It was the morning of the third day that I fell under suspicion. Irrevocably, as it turned out. "I think we're ignoring the new people," said Roberta Jar. "I've seen it again and again, some newcomer draws the mafia card and sits there, playing innocent and silent, just mowing the village down while we argue. I think we ought to look at Joel, for instance. He isn't saying *anything*."

"I heard him talking to Doe," someone volunteered. "They have some little thing going on the side."

"Both mafia, then," said one of the leader men, whose every pronouncement was full of unearned certainty. "Take them both out."

"I'm a villager," I said. This was the standard protest, despite its deep meaninglessness: Who wouldn't say that?

Someone laughed at me sharply for being unpersuasive. Before I'd assembled a better defense, hands shot up all around the circle. Even Doe voted for my banishment.

Adam Cressner then shepherded the village into night. "The dead usually wander off where they can talk without disturbing the village," he stage-whispered across their bowed heads. I took the hint. As I moved into the hall, Adam returned to narration: "Mafia, open your eyes, and silently agree on someone to kill—" I wondered who the dastards were.

The zombies who'd vacated the parlor were gathered out on the brownstone's stoop, smoking cigarettes and gabbling. They spotted me peering through the front door's doubled glass panes. I made a gesture meant to be interpretable as *Be right there, just going for a pee*. Someone waved back. I went downstairs.

The half-basement's front room was furnished as a suburban den, with a stereo and large-screen TV, and walls lined with CDs, laser discs, and books, many of them expensive museum catalogues, compendiums of film stills, photo-essays from boutique imprints. I spotted a brightly colored paperback on a shelf of oversized volumes on art and antiquities: *Origins*, by Stan Lee, a reprint compendium of comic books introducing various Marvel characters: Spider-Man, Iron Man, the Fantastic Four. A sequel, *Son of Origins*, was shelved beside it. I browsed both, but the Vision wasn't included. He wasn't the sort of character who'd had such a prominent debut—more of a cult figure, I recalled. Like Rhoda or Fraser, he'd been an unplanned star, spun from an ensemble.

The pop-art panels looked thin and fraudulent on white paper, instead of the soft, yellowed rag of the old comics from which they'd been reprinted. Nevertheless, I felt a howling nostalgia rise in me at the sight of the Silver Surfer and Daredevil, characters who'd meant a tremendous amount to me for a brief moment in junior high, then been utterly forgotten. I'd discovered Marvel Comics a year or two after leaving P.S. 29 and Adam Cressner behind. The oddness of Adam's choice in identifying with the Vision had had a troubling chicken-or-egg quality to me then—did the character seem so depressed and diffident to me *because* of Adam's red face paint? The answer wasn't in *Origins*, or *Son of Origins*.

I replaced the books on the shelf and went digging in the walk-in closet instead.

"Hello?" Someone had entered the room behind me. It was Doe, swinging a beer bottle elegantly by the neck.

"Oh, hi," I said.

"What are you doing?"

"Looking for something."

"Something?"

"A costume, or a cape," I said. "It's a long story." I emerged from the closet, which seemed to hold only wool coats and ski gear anyway. "Did you get voted out of the village?"

"Right after you."

"Sorry. I guess I dragged us both down with that suspicious side talk. A rookie mistake."

"It's okay. They were right to. I was in the mafia."

"Ah. Now I feel truly foolish."

"Don't. It was brave of you to speak up at all. The first time I played I just cowered." Her tiny mouth was perfect apart from one incisor that seemed to have been inserted sideways for variation, like a domino.

"How do you know Adam and Roberta?"

"Adam was my dissertation adviser. At Columbia." Doe squinted at me oddly, expectantly, perhaps sensing I didn't know the first thing about Adam. She was right and wrong, of course.

"I'm just the friendly neighbor," I said. I considered how the word *friendly* could mean *not an actual friend*— like friendish, or friendlike. "Is this a whole, ah, Columbia group, upstairs?" I wondered what the man who'd been the Vision would teach: Android identity politics?

"Just that guy Barth who got killed. The rest I don't know. Adam and Roberta seem to collect people from all over the place."

"They're not big on introductions, are they? They prefer keeping everyone in the dark, and dependent on them."

"Maybe they figure we're grown-ups and can take care of ourselves."

I'd touched the limits of Doe's disloyalty, and been admonished. I rather liked it. "Yes, of course," I agreed. "The way we are, now, for instance. You and I, I mean. Taking care of ourselves."

Doe only blinked, as when, in the circle upstairs, I'd probed her mafia status.

There commenced a clunking and scraping of chairs above our heads. The village had shrunk, or dissolved. I stepped forward and took Doe's hand, thinking I only had a minute. I had less, as it happened. For a giantess Roberta Jar moved silently, and now she was in the doorway. Doe's hand slipped from mine as a newt darts from view on a forest path.

"Game over?" I asked.

"Yes," said Roberta, cat-ate-canaryishly. "The mafia won."

"The mafia always wins," said Doe, a little petulantly, I thought, given her own affiliation.

"Not really," said Roberta. "But they have had their way recently, it's true."

"They did fine without *my* help," mused Doe. This accounted for her bitterness: she'd wanted to prove essential.

We returned upstairs on a quest for more beer. The smokers had returned from the stoop, and villagers and mafia alike mingled in excited dissection of the game's plot: *I told you so* was the general thrust. There was hopeful talk of another game, but Val and Irene, a couple with babysitter problems, had to go. A few more defections followed, and suddenly we didn't have numbers enough for a village. "Don't everybody go," said Adam, as one after another made their excuses. "The night is young."

Seven of us remained. Happily, this included Doe. There were also two younger men vying for the attention of an Asian woman named Flour. Perhaps predictably, it was singles who'd stayed—us with nothing to rush home to. We sat in the sea of empty bottles and abandoned chairs, a ghost village. But Adam Cressner and Roberta Jar seemed glad to have us. He went downstairs and soon Chet Baker emanated from speakers in the parlor's corners. Roberta lowered the lights.

"I know a game," I said.

"Yes?" said Roberta.

"It's called I Never. It's a drinking game, though. We all have to have an alcoholic beverage in our hands."

Adam plopped two fresh sixes of Pale Ale at our feet. I explained the rules: Each of us in turn made a statement— a true statement—beginning with the words *I never*. Those in the circle who'd done the things the speaker hadn't were required to confess their experience, by sipping their beer. Thus the worldly among us were made to grow embarrassed, and intoxicated, and thus secrets were flushed into the open.

"For example, I'll start," I said. "I've never had sex on an airplane."

Adam and Roberta smiled at one another and tipped their bottles. Flour also wet her lips, and one of her suitors as well. Doe and the second of Flour's men were in my more innocent camp.

"Excellent," I said. "The rest is just a matter of thinking of good questions." I felt now an unexpectedly sharp appetite for this game—I wanted Adam and Roberta, and Doe too, to see how false the drama of Mafia was compared to our real lives. Of course, after my example we first had to endure a tentative round of inquiries into sex on trains, in restaurant coatrooms, in film projection booths, etc. When my turn came again I ratcheted things up a notch.

"I've never had sex with anyone in this room," I said.

Adam and Roberta clinked bottles, toasting smug coupledom.

Then Doe raised her drink and gulped, eyes closed. "*Oooh*," said one of the single men. I did the easy math, then inspected Roberta for her reaction. If anything, she looked ready to toast Doe's confession as well. Certainly it came as no surprise.

"I've . . . never . . ." Flour thought hard, eager to fill the loud silence. We were eager to have her fill it. "I've . . . never . . . had sex with a married person."

"Good one," congratulated one of her suitors.

I was forced to drink to this, as were our sybaritic hosts—and, yes, Doe. Her long-lashed eyes remained cast down to the floor, or squeezed as if in pain.

It was Adam's turn. "I've never killed anything bigger than a cockroach," he said.

Neither had I. Nor Roberta Jar, nor the woman named Flour or her two wannabe boyfriends. No, it was Doe again who had been trapped by the odd question, who raised her bottle once more to her thin-pressed lips. I wasn't sure she actually drank, but I wasn't about to call her on it.

It's the nature of I Never, as in other of life's arenas,

that though explanations aren't called for in the rules one often feels compelled to explain. I can't claim our circle didn't look to Doe for some gloss on her lonely confession.

"I was five," she began, and there was something ominous in the specificity: not *four or five*, or *five or six*. "My uncle had given me a new kitten, and I was playing alone in the yard with it, with some string. I hadn't even given the kitten a name yet." Doe looked at Adam Cressner, as if the whole game had devolved to the authority of his eerie question. "There was a tree in the yard, it's still there"—she spoke as though hypnotized, and seeing the tree float before her—"my parents still have the house. I used to climb the tree, and I had the idea I would take the kitten up the tree with me. I tied the string around the kitten's neck"—here Flour gasped—"and tried to pulley it up with me, across a branch."

Her tale's Clint Eastwoodian climax having been telegraphed by Adam's question, Doe was permitted a graceful elision. "A neighbor saw the whole thing from a window across the yard. He thought I'd done it on purpose, and he told my parents."

"Did they believe you?" asked Roberta Jar, clinically impassive.

"I don't know," said Doe, raising her eyebrows. "It didn't matter, really. Every since then I think something broke inside me . . . when my parents made me understand that the kitten wasn't alive anymore . . . there's always been a part of me missing."

"That's *horrible*," said one of Flour's men.

"I mean, I still have a capacity for happiness," said Doe, matter-of-factly, almost impatiently. It was as though she wanted to protect us from her story now, felt bad for telling it.

We meditated in silence on what we'd learned. Someone guzzled their beer, not as a gesture within the game, just to do it: a quiet pop of bottle mouth unsealing from lips was audible in a break between songs, Chet Baker finishing "I Fall in Love Too Easily," then, absurdly, beginning "Everything Happens to Me." I'd have been tempted to put my arm around Doe's shoulders, or even lead her from the room, if she as much as met my eye. She didn't. Tears streaked Flour's ivory cheeks instead.

Adam Cressner began speaking. At first it seemed a hollow gambit, an attempt to distract us from Doe's testimony by non sequitur. "When I was last in Germany, I visited the Glyptotek in Munich," he said. "It's full of statuary the Europeans ripped out of the old temples. They've got a Roman copy of a Greek marble by Boëthus—the original's in the Vatican—showing a boy with a goose. The bird's practically as big as the boy, and they're wrestling. The kid's got the goose by the neck. A museum guard came up behind me, he saw I was transfixed by this sculpture, and he uttered this line I'll never forget, it shot through me like a bolt: 'Spielend, doch, mit toedlichem Griff.' *He thinks it's a game, but he's choking the goose.* But in the guard's High German it was more allusive and grand—'playing, but with a deadly grip.' "

"Like something from Rilke," said Roberta Jar.

Oh yes, I thought viciously, *Rilke* and *High German* after four or five beers. You're both such fine people. However slow my uptake, a picture formed: I now supposed Doe's dissertation had been in art history, for example. And that Adam Cressner and Roberta Jar had together known, from intimate experience, how easily Doe might be induced to turn herself inside out for us.

I wanted revenge on Doe's behalf. "I've never," I said loudly.

All stared. I began again. "I've never pretended I was a character from a comic book. Never, say, dressed up in a superhero costume, not even on Halloween." I glared at Adam Cressner: Let him eat cape.

It was Roberta Jar who drew our attention, though, by lifting her bottle high, as if to toast again before she sipped. We looked to her as we had to Doe.

"I met a man once," Roberta said. "I liked this man, well, very, very much. This was eight years ago now." She lolled her big head, a little shy to tell it, though her voice was still strong and resonant in her chest. "When we began to see one another, this man and I, there was something between us that was difficult, a secret—a secret priority in his life. It had to do with this, exactly: dressing up as a character from a comic book. And this priority was difficult for both of us."

She'd turned my hostile joke into another confession, to give Doe company. We listened wide-eyed—I caught Flour glancing at me, likely wondering how I'd known to ask the question, as I'd wondered before at Adam Cressner. As for Adam, he sat quietly adoring his paramour while she spilled on.

"I realized I had to learn as much about this as I could, or it would beat us, and I was determined not to be beaten. I discovered that the comic-book character in question had gotten married, to another character, called the Scarlet Witch. I thought this was very unusual, two married superheroes, and I took it as a good sign. So, I went shopping for fabric, and hand-sewed a Scarlet Witch costume. Tights, and pink boots, a sort of pink headpiece to hold back my hair. I did a good job, really impressed myself. It was the most sustained arts-and-crafts project of my life, actually."

Roberta paused, and in the silence we were allowed to sense the result of her efforts, a climax as inevitable and in its way as horrible as the kitten's execution. I wondered if Adam still wore the red food coloring for face paint, or whether he'd found some better method, easier to remove when he'd wanted to pass for a mere Columbia professor. I thought of the Scarlet Witch as I knew her from Marvel Comics, an exotic beauty whose powers, loosely defined as "sorcery," mostly consisted of throwing up pink force fields, but whose real achievement was a stoical, unwavering devotion to her Spock-like emotional mute of a husband.

I looked again to Adam Cressner. I still faintly wished for the satisfaction of an unmasking, but his eyes gave me nothing. Adam Cressner was as little interested in my impressions of his Visionhood as he'd been at second base, all those years ago. He hadn't even sipped his beer to confess the truth.

"I have to go," said Doe suddenly. She flinched her head from me, from all of us, hastily gathered a load of beer bottles into the kitchen and rinsed them in the sink. I wondered if she'd also been enticed into a costume—Ant-Girl, or Thumbelina.

"Well, anyway, that's my story," said Roberta, the sardonic twang restored to her voice. One of the men gave an artificial laugh, barely adequate to break the tension. It was only now that Adam Cressner followed the game's protocol and also drank. I'd had my answer, though not as I'd wanted it, from Adam's mouth. I don't even know whether Flour or the two men had any understanding of what had happened—for all Roberta had told us, the man in question could have been someone other than Adam. Strangely, it was as if he and I were allies, having each forced confession from the other's woman. Except that neither woman was mine, and both might be his.

"A beautiful story it is," said Adam Cressner. "With that we'll see our dear guests to the door, yes?"

No one resisted. The spell was broken. We were in some way broken, shattered by the game, unable to recover any sense of delight in one another's company, if we'd ever had that—I no longer knew. We cleared bottles, shuffled chairs, mumbled excuses, made promises to be in touch, to forward one another's e-mail addresses, which rang hollow. Within ten minutes we were out on the street, each

headed home alone. At least I think we were alone. Certainly Doe strolled away, apart from the others, a tiny figure vanishing on the pavement, before I'd turned my back
and descended into my basement entrance, before I'd even
had a chance to wish her good night or kiss her equivo-
cally on the cheek. It's possible one of Flour's suitors followed her home, but I doubt it. It had all been a little much
for us poor singles, the tyranny of the Vision and the Scarlet Witch.

Access Fantasy

THERE WAS A START-UP ABOUT A HALF MILE ahead the day before, a fever of distant engines and horns honking as others signaled their excitement—a chance to move!—and so he'd spent the day jammed behind the wheel, living in his Apartment on Tape, waiting for that chance, listening under the drone of distant helicopters to hear the start-up make its way downtown. But the wave of revving engines stalled before reaching his street. He never even saw a car move, just heard them. In fact he couldn't remember seeing a car move recently. Perhaps the start-up was only a panic begun by someone warming their motor, reviving their battery. That night he'd dreamed another start-up, or perhaps it was real, a far-off flare that died before he'd even ground the sleep out of his eyes, though in the rustle of his waking thoughts it was a perfect thing, coordinated, a dance of cars shifting through the free-flowing streets. Dream or not, either way, didn't matter. He fell back asleep. What woke him in the morning was the family in the Pacer up ahead cooking breakfast. They had a stove on the roof of their car and the dad was grilling something they'd bought from the flatbed shepherd two blocks away, a sheepsteak or something. It smelled good. Everything about the family in the Pacer made him too conscious of his wants. The family's daughter—she was beautiful—had been working as Advertising, pushing up against and through the One-Way Permeable Barrier on behalf of some vast faceless corporation. That being the only way through the One-Way Permeable Barrier, of course. So the family, her ma and pa, were flush, had dough, and vendors knew to seek them out, hawking groceries. Whereas checking his pockets he didn't have more than a couple of dollars. There was a coffee-and-doughnuts man threading his way through the traffic even now but coffee was beyond his means. He needed money. Rumors had it Welfare Helicopters had been sighted south of East One Thousand, One Hundred and Ninety-Fourth Street, and a lot of people had left their cars, drifted down that way, looking for easy cash. Which was one reason the start-up died, it occurred to him—too many empty cars. Along with the cars that wouldn't start anymore, like the old lady in the Impala beside him, the dodderer. She'd given up, spent most days dozing in the backseat. Her nephew from a few blocks away came over and tinkered with her engine now and again but it wasn't helping. It just meant the nephew wasn't at his wheel for the start-up, another dead spot, another reason not to bother waiting to move. Probably he thought now he should have walked downtown himself in search of welfare money drifting down from the sky. The state helicopters weren't coming around this neighborhood much lately. Alas. The air was crowded with commercial hovercraft instead, recruiters, Advertising robots rounding up the girl from the Pacer and others like her, off to the world on the other side of the One-Way Permeable Barrier, however briefly. The world of apartments, real ones. Though it was morning he went back to his latest Apartment on Tape, which was a four-bedroom two-bath co-op on East One Thousand, Two Hundred and Fifteenth Street, just a few blocks away but another world of course, remote from his life on the street, sealed off from it by the One-Way Permeable Barrier. He preferred the early part of the tape, before any of the furnishings arrived, so he rewound to that part and put the tape on slow and lived in the rooms as hard as he could, ignoring the glare of sun through his windshield that dulled his view of the dashboard television, ignoring the activities of the family in the Pacer up ahead as they clambered in and out of the hatchback, ignoring the clamor of his own pangs. The realtor's voice was annoying, it was a squawking, parroty voice so he kept the volume down as always and lived in the rooms silently, letting his mind sweep in and haunt the empty spaces, the rooms unfolding in slow motion for the realtor's camera. While the camera lingered in the bathroom he felt under his seat for his bottle and unzipped and peed, timed so it matched to the close-up of the automatic flushing of the toilet on his television. Then the camera and his attention wandered out into the hall. That's when he noticed it, the shadow. Just for a moment. He rewound to see it again. On the far wall of the hallway, framed perfectly for an instant in the lens, was the silhouette of a struggle, a man with his hands on the neck of another, smaller. A woman. Shaking her by the neck for that instant, before the image vanished. Like a pantomime of murder, a Punch-and-Judy show hidden in the Apartment on Tape. But real, it had to be real. Why hadn't he noticed before? He'd watched this tape dozens of times. He rewound again. Just barely, but still. Unmistakable, however brief. The savagery of it was awful. If only he could watch it frame by frame—slow motion was disastrously fast now. Who was the killer? The landlord? The realtor? Why? Was the victim the previous tenant? Questions, he had questions. He felt himself begin to buzz with them, come alive. Slow motion didn't seem particularly slow precisely because his attention had quickened. Yes, a job of detection was just what he needed to roust himself out of the current slump, burn off the torpor of too many days locked in the jam at the same damn intersection— why hadn't he gone downtown at that last turnoff, months ago? Well, anyway. He watched it again, memorized the shadow, the silhouette, imagined blurred features in the slurry of video fuzz, memorized the features, what the hell. Like a police sketch, work from his own prescient hallucinations. Again. It grew sharper every time. He'd scrape a hole in this patch of tape, he knew, if he rewound too many times. Better to have the tape, the evidence, all there was at this point. He popped the video, threw it in a satchel with notebook, eyeglasses. Extra socks. Outside, locked the car, tipped an imaginary hat at the old lady, headed east by foot on West One Thousand, Two Hundred and Eighth Street. He had to duck uptown two blocks to avoid a flotilla of Sanitation hovertrucks spraying foamy water to wash cars sealed up tight against this artificial rain but also soaking poor jerks asleep, drenching interiors, the rotted upholstery and split spongy dashboards, extinguishing rooftop bonfires, destroying box gardens, soap bubbles poisoning the feeble sprouts. Children screamed and giggled, the streets ran with water, sluicing shit here and there into drains, more often along under the tires to the unfortunate neighboring blocks, everyone moaning and lifting their feet clear. Just moving it around, that's all. At the next corner he ran into a crowd gathered staring at a couple of young teenage girls from inside, from the apartments, the other side of the barrier. They'd come out of the apartment building on rollerblades to sightsee, to slum on the streets. Sealed in a murky bubble of the One-Way Permeable Barrier they were like apparitions, dim ghosts, though you could hear them giggle as they skated through the hushed, reverent crowd. Like a sighting of gods, these teenage girls from inside. No one bothered to spare-change them or bother them in any way because of the barrier. The girls of course were oblivious behind their twilight veil, like night things come into the day, though for them probably it was the people in cars and around the cars that appeared dim, unreachable. He shouldered his way through the dumbstruck crowd and once past this obstacle he found his man, locked into traffic like all the rest, right where he'd last seen him. The Apartments on Tape dealer, his connection, sunbathing in a deck chair on the roof of his Sentra, eating a sandwich. The backseat was stacked with realtors' tapes, apartment porn, and on the passenger seat two video decks for dubbing. His car in a sliver of morning sun that shone across the middle of the block, benefit of a chink in the canyon of towers that surrounded them. The dealer's neighbors were on their car roofs as well, stretching in the sun, drying clothes. "Hello there, remember me? That looks good what you're eating, anyway, I want to talk to you about this tape." "No refunds," said the dealer, not even looking down. "No, that's not it, I saw something, can we watch it together?" "No need since there's no refunds and I'm hardly interested—" "Listen, this is a police matter, I think—" "You're police then, is that what you're saying?" still not looking down. "No no, I fancy myself a private detective, though not to say I work outside the law, more adjacent, then turn it over to them if it serves justice, there's so often corruption—" "So turn it over," the dealer said. "Well if you could just have a look I'd value your opinion. Sort of pick your brain," thinking flattery or threats, should have chosen one approach with this guy, stuck with it. The dealer said, "Sorry, day off," still not turning his head, chewing off another corner of sandwich. Something from inside the sandwich fell, a chunk of something, fish maybe, onto the roof of the car. "The thing is I think I saw a murder, on the tape, in the apartment." "That's highly unlikely." "I know, but that's what I saw." "Murder, huh?" The dealer didn't sound at all impressed. "Bloody body parts, that sort of thing?" "No, don't be absurd, just a shadow, just a trace." "Hmmm." "You never would have noticed in passing. Hey, come to think of it, you don't have an extra sandwich do you?" "No, I don't. So would you describe this shadow as sort of a flicker then, like a malfunction?" "No, absolutely not. It's part of the tape." "Not your monitor on the fritz?" "No"—he was getting angry now—"a person, a shadow strangling another shadow." The chunk of sandwich filling on the car roof was sizzling slightly, changing color already in the sun. The dealer said, "Shadows, hmmm. Probably a gimmick, subliminal special effects or something." "What? What reason would a realtor have for adding special effects for God's sake to an apartment tape?" "Maybe they think it adds some kind of allure, some thrill of menace that makes their apartments stand out from the crowd." "I doubt very much—" "Maybe they've become aware of the black market in tapes lately, that's the word on the street in fact, and so they're trying to send a little message. They don't like us ogling their apartments, even vicariously." "You can't ogle vicariously,

I think. Sounds wrong. Anyway, that's the most ridiculous thing I've ever—" "Or maybe I'm in on it, maybe I'm the killer, have you considered that?" "Now you're making fun of me." "Why? If you can solve crimes on the other side of the barrier why can't I commit them?" The dealer laughed, hyena-like. "Now seriously," he continued, "if you want to exchange for one without a murder I'll give you a credit toward the next, half what you paid—" "No thanks. I'll hold on to it." Discouraged, hungry, but he couldn't really bother being angry. What help did he expect from the dealer anyway? This was a larger matter, above the head of a mere middleman. "Good luck, Sherlock," the dealer was saying. "Spread word freely, by the way, don't hold back. Can't hurt my sales any. People like murder, only it might be good if there was skin instead of only shadow, a tit say." "Yes, very good then, appreciate your help. Carry on." The dealer saluted. He saluted back, started off through the traffic, stomach growling, ignoring it, intent. A killer was at large. Weaving past kids terrorizing an entire block of cars with an elaborate tag game, cornering around the newly washed neighborhood now wringing itself out, muddy streams between the cars and crying babies ignoring vendors with items he couldn't afford and a flatbed farmer offering live kittens for pets or food and a pathetic miniature start-up, three cars idiotically nosing rocking jerking back and forth trying to rearrange themselves pointlessly, one of them now sideways wheels on the curb and nobody else even taking the bait he made his way back to his car and key in the lock noticed the girl from the

Pacer standing in her red dress on the hood of the car gazing skyward, waiting for the Advertising people to take her
away. Looking just incidentally like a million bucks. Her
kid brother was away, maybe part of the gang playing tag,
and her parents were inside the car doing housework Dad
scraping the grill out the window Mom airing clothes
repacking bundles so he went over, suddenly inspired.
"Margaret, isn't it?" She nodded, smiled. "Yes, good, well
you remember me from next door, I'm looking for a day or
two's work and do you think they'll take me along?" She
said, "You never know, they just take you or they don't."
Smiling graciously even if a little confused, neighbors so
long and they'd never spoken. "But you always—" he began pointing out. She said, "Oh once they've started taking you then—" Awkwardly, they were both awkward for
a moment not saying what they both knew or at least he
did, that she was an attractive young girl and likely that
made a huge difference in whether they wanted you. "Well
you wouldn't mind if I tried?" he said and she said, "No,
no," relieved almost, then added, "I can point you out, I
can suggest to them—" Now he was embarrassed and said
hurriedly, "That's so good of you, thanks, and where
should I wait, not here with you at your folks' car, I
guess—" "Why not, climb up." Dad looked out the door
up at them and she waved him off. "It's okay, you know
him from next door he's going to work, we're going to try
to get him a job Advertising." "Okay, sweetheart, just
checking on you." Then she grabbed his arm, said,
"Look." The Advertising hovercraft she'd been watching

for landed on the curb a half block ahead, near the giant hideous sculpture at an office building main entrance, lately sealed. Dad said, "Get going you guys, and good luck," and she said, "C'mon." Such neighborliness was a surprise since he'd always felt shut out by the family in the Pacer but obviously it was in his head. And Margaret, a cloud of good feeling seemed to cover her. No wonder they wanted her for Advertising. "Hurry," she said and took his hand and they hopped down and pushed their way around the cars and through the chaos of children and barking dogs and vendors trying to work the crowd of wannabes these landings always provoked, to join the confused throng at the entrance. He held on to his satchel with the video and his socks making sure it didn't get picked in this crowd. She bounced there trying to make herself visible until one of the two robots at the door noticed her and pointed. They stepped up. "Inside," said the robot. They were ugly little robots with their braincases undisguised and terrible attitudes. He disliked them instantly. "I brought someone new," she said, pulling him by the hand, thrusting him into view. "Yes, sir, I'd like to enlist—" he started, grinning madly, wanting to make a good impression. The robot looked him over and made its rapid-fire assessment, nodded. "Get inside," it said. "Lucky," she whispered, and they stepped into the hovercraft. Four others were there, two men, two women, all young. And another woman stumbled in behind them, and the door sealed, and they were off. Nasty little robots scurrying into the cockpit, making things ready. "Now what?"

he said and she put her finger to her lips and shushed him, but sweetly, leaning into him as if to say they were in this together. He wanted to tell her what he was after but the robots might hear. Would they care? Yes, no, he couldn't know. Such ugly, fascistic little robots. Nazi robots, that's what they were. He hated placing himself in their hands. But once he was Advertising he would be through the barrier, he'd be able to investigate. Probably he should keep his assignment to himself, though. He didn't want to get her into trouble. The hovercraft shuddered, groaned, then lifted and through the window he could see the cars growing smaller, his neighborhood, his life, the way the traffic was so bad for hundreds of miles of street and why did he think a start-up would change anything? Was there a place where cars really drove anymore? Well, anyway. The robots were coming around with the Advertising Patches and everyone leaned their heads forward obediently, no first-timers like himself apparently. He did the same. A robot fastened a patch behind his right ear, a moment of stinging skin, nothing more. Hard to believe the patch was enough to interfere with the function of the One-Way Permeable Barrier, that he would now be vivid and tangible and effective to those on the other side. "I don't feel any different," he whispered. "You won't," she said, "not until there's people. Then you'll be compelled to Advertise. You won't be able to help it." "For what, though?" "You never know, coffee, diamonds, condoms, vacations, you just never know." "Where—" "They'll drop us off at the Undermall, then we're on our own." "Will we be able to stick

together?" The question was out before he could wonder
if it was presuming too much, but she said, "Sure, as long
as our products aren't too incompatible, but we'll know
soon. Anyway, just follow me." She really had a warmth, a
glow. Incompatible products? Well, he'd find out what that
meant. The hovercraft bumped down on the roof of a
building, and with grim efficiency the ugly Nazi robots
had the door open and were marching the conscripts out
to a rooftop elevator. He wanted to reach out and smack
their little exposed-braincase heads together. But he had to
keep his cool, stay undercover. He trotted across the roof
toward the elevator after her, between the rows of offi-
cious gesticulating robots, like they were going to a con-
centration camp. The last robot at the door of the elevator
handed them each an envelope before they stepped in. He
took his and moved into the corner with Margaret, they
were really packing them in but he couldn't complain actually being jostled with her and she didn't seem to be trying to avoid it. He poked into the envelope. It was full of
bills, singles mostly. The money was tattered and filthy,
bills that had been taken out of circulation on the other
side of the barrier. Garbage money, that's what it was. The
others had already pocketed theirs, business as usual apparently. "Why do they pay us now?" he whispered. She
said, "We just find our way out at the end, when the patch
runs out, so this way they don't have to deal with us
again," and he said, "What if we just took off with the
money?" "You could I guess, but I've never seen anyone do
it since you'd never get to come back and anyway the

patch makes you really want to Advertise, you'll see." Her voice was reassuring, like she really wanted him not to worry and he felt rotten not telling her about his investigation, his agenda. He put the envelope into his satchel with tape and socks. The elevator sealed and whooshed them down through the building, into the Undermall, then the doors opened and they unpacked from the elevator, spewed out into a gigantic lobby, all glass and polished steel with music playing softly and escalators going down and up in every direction, escalators with steps of burnished wood that looked good enough to eat, looked like roast chicken. He was still so hungry. Margaret took his hand again. "Let's go," she said. As the others dispersed she led him toward one of the escalators and they descended. The corridor below branched to shops with recessed entrances, windows dark and smoky, quiet pulsing music fading from each door, also food smells here and there causing his saliva to flow, and holographic signs angling into view as they passed: FERN SLAW, ROETHKE AND SONS, HOLLOW APPEAL, BROKEN SMUDGED ALPHABET, BURGER KING, PLASTIC DEVILS, OSTRICH LAKE, SMARTINGALE'S, RED HARVEST, CATCH OF THE DAY, MUTUAL OF FOMALHAUT, THNEEDS, etcetera. She led him on, confidently, obviously at home. Why not, this was what she did with her days. Then without warning, a couple appeared from around a corner, and he felt himself begin to Advertise. "How do you do today?" he said, sidling up to the gentleman of the couple, even as he saw Margaret begin to do the same thing to the lady. The gentleman nodded at him, walked on. But met his eye. He was tangible, he could be heard. It was a shock. "Thirsty?" he heard himself say. "How long's it been since you had a nice refreshing beer?" "Don't like beer," said the gentleman. "Can't say why, just never have." "Then you've obviously never tried a Very Old Money Lager," he heard himself say, still astonished. The barrier was pierced and he was conversing, he was perceptible. He'd be able to conduct interrogations, be able to search out clues. Meanwhile he heard Margaret saying, "Don't demean your signature with a second-rate writing implement. Once you've tried the Eiger fountain pen you'll never want to go back to those henlike scratchings and scrawlings," and the woman seemed interested and so Margaret went on "our Empyrean Sterling Silver Collection features one-of-a-kind hand-etched casings—" In fact the man seemed captivated too. He turned ignoring the beer pitch and gave Margaret his attention. "Our brewers handpick the hops and malt," he was unable to stop though he'd obviously lost his mark, "and every single batch of fire-brewed Very Old Money Lager is individually tasted—" Following the couple through the corridor they bumped into another Advertising woman who'd been on the hovercraft, and she began singing, "Vis-it the *moon*, it's nev-er too *soon*," dancing sinuously and batting her eyes, distracting them all from fountain pens and beer for the moment and then the five of them swept into the larger space of the Undermall and suddenly there were dozens of people who needed to be told about the beer. "Thirsty? Hello, hi there, thirsty? Excuse me, thirsty? Yes?

Craving satisfaction, sparkle, bite? No? Yes? Have you
tried Very Old Money? What makes it different, you ask—
oh, hello, thirsty?" and also dozens of people working
as Advertising, a gabble of pitches—stern, admonitory:
"Have you considered the perils of being without success
insurance?"; flippant, arbitrary: "You never know you're
out with the Black Underwear Crowd, not until you get
one of them home!"; jingly, singsong: "We've got children,
we've all got children, you can have children too—" and as
they scattered and darted along the endless marble floors
of the Undermall he was afraid he'd lose her, but there was
Margaret, earnestly discussing pens with a thoughtful
older couple and he struggled over toward her, hawking
beer—"Thirsty? Oof, sorry, uh, thirsty?" The crowd
thinned as customers ducked into shops and stole away
down corridors back to their apartments, bullied by the
slew of Advertising except for the few like this older couple who seemed gratified by the attention, he actually had
to wait as they listened and took down some information
from Margaret about the Eiger fountain pen while he
stood far enough away to keep from barking at them
about the beer. Then once the older couple wandered off
he took Margaret's hand this time, why not, she'd done it,
and drew her down a corridor away from the crowds, hoping to keep from engaging with any more customers, and
also in the right direction if he had his bearings. He
thought he did. He led her into the shadow of a doorway,
a shop called Fingertoes that wasn't doing much business.
"Listen, I've got to tell you something, I haven't been com-

pletely truthful, I mean, I haven't lied, but there's something—" She looked at him, hopeful, confused, but gener-
ous in her interpretation, he could tell, what a pure and
sweet disposition, maybe her dad wasn't such a bad guy
after all if he'd raised a plum like this. "I'm a detective, I
mean, what does that mean, really, but the thing is there's
been a murder and I'm trying to look into it—" and then
he plunged in and told all, the Apartment on Tape, pulling
it out of his satchel to show her, the shadow, the strangling, his conversation with the dealer and then his brain-
storm to slip inside the citadel, slip past the One-Way
Permeable Barrier that would of course have kept his questions or accusations from even being audible to those on
this side, and so he'd manipulated her generosity to get
aboard the hovercraft. "Forgive me," he said. Her eyes
widened, her voice grew hushed, reverent. "Of course, but
what do you want to do? Find the police?" "You're not angry at me?" "No, no. It's a brave thing you're doing."
"Thank you." They drew closer. He could almost kiss her,
just in happiness, solidarity, no further meaning or if there
was it was just on top of the powerful solidarity feeling,
just an extra, a windfall. "But what do you think is best,
the police?" she whispered. "No, I have in mind a visit to
the apartment, we're only a couple of blocks away, in this
direction I believe, but do you think we can get upstairs?"
They fell silent then because a man swerved out of Fingertoes with a little paper tray of greasy fried things, looked
like fingers or toes in fact and smelled terrific, he couldn't
believe how hungry he was. "Thirsty?" he said hopelessly

and the man popping one into his mouth said, "You called it, brother, I'm dying for a beer." "Why just any beer when you could enjoy a Very Old Money—" and he had to go on about it, being driven nuts by the smell, while Margaret waited. The moment the grease-eater realized they were Advertising and broke free, toward the open spaces of the Undermall, he and Margaret broke in the other direction, down the corridor. "This way," said Margaret, turning them toward the elevator, "the next level down you can go for blocks, it's the way out eventually too." "Yes, but can we get back upstairs?" "The elevators work for us until the patches run out, I think," and so they went down below the Undermall to the underground corridors, long echoey halls of tile, not so glamorous as upstairs, not nice at all really, the lengths apartment people went never to have to step out onto the street and see car people being really appalling sometimes. The tunnels were marked with street signs, names of other Undermalls, here and there an exit. They had to Advertise only once before reaching East One Thousand, Two Hundred and Fifteenth Street, to a group of teenage boys smoking a joint in the corridor who laughed and asked Margaret questions she couldn't answer like are they mightier or less mighty than the sword and do they work for pigs. They ran into another person Advertising, a man moving furtively who when he recognized Margaret was plainly relieved. "He's got a girlfriend," she explained, somewhat enigmatically. So those Advertising could, did—what? Interact. But caught up in the chase now, he didn't ask more, just counted the blocks, feeling the thrill of approaching his Apartment on Tape's real address. They went up in the elevator, which was lavish again, wood paneled and perfumed and mirrored and musical. An expensive building. Apartment 16D. So he pressed the button for the sixteenth floor, holding his breath, hardly believing it when they rose above the public floors. But they did. He gripped her hand. The elevator stopped on the sixth floor and a robot got on. Another of the creepily efficient braincase-showing kind. At first the robot ignored them but then on the fifteenth floor a woman got on and Margaret said, "The most personal thing about you is your signature, don't you think?" and he said, "Thirsty?" and the robot turned and stared up at them. The doors closed and they rode up to the sixteenth floor, and the three of them got out, he and Margaret and the robot, leaving the woman behind. The hallway was splendid with plush carpeting and brass light fixtures, empty apart from the three of them. "What are you doing up here?" said the robot. "And what's in that bag?" Clutching his satchel he said, "Nothing, just my stuff." "Why is it any of your business?" said Margaret, surprisingly defiant. "We've been asked to give an extended presentation at a customer's private home," he said, wanting quickly to cover Margaret's outburst, give the robot something else to focus on. "Then I'll escort you," said the robot. "You really don't have to do that," he said. "Don't come along and screw up our pitch, we'll sue you," Margaret added bizarrely. Learning of the investigation had an odd effect on her, always a risk working with amateurs he supposed. But also it was these robots, the way they were designed with rotten personalities or no personalities they really aroused revulsion in people, it was an instinctual thing and not just him, he noted with satisfaction. He squeezed her hand and said, "Our sponsors would be displeased, it's true." "This matter requires clearance," said the robot, trying to get in front of them as they walked, and they had to skip to stay ahead of it. "Please stand to one side and wait for clearance," but they kept going down the carpeted hallway, his fingers crossed that it was the right direction for 16D. "Halt," said the robot, a flashing red light on its forehead beginning to blink neurotically and then they were at the door, and he rapped with his knuckles, thinking, hardly going incognito here, but better learn what we can. "Stand to one side," said the robot again. "Shut up," said Margaret. As the robot clamped a steely hand on each of their arms, jerking them back away from the door, its treads grinding on the carpet for traction, probably leaving ugly marks too, the door swung open. "Hello?" The man in the doorway was unshaven and slack-haired wearing a robe and blinking at them as though he'd only turned on his light to answer the door. "They claim to have an appointment with you, sir," said the robot. The man only stood and stared. "It's very important, we have to talk to you urgently," he said, trying to pull free of the robot's chilly grip, then added, regretfully, "about beer." He felt a swoon at looking through the doorway, realizing he was seeing into his Apartment on Tape, the rooms etched into his dreamy brain now before

him. He tried to see more but the light was gloomy. "And
fountain pens," said Margaret, obviously trying to hold
herself back but compelled to chip in something. "I apologize, sir, I tried to detain them to obtain clearance—" said
the robot. *Detain, obtain*, what rotten syntax, he thought,
the people who program these robots certainly aren't
poets. The man just stood and blinked and looked them
over, the three of them struggling subtly, he and Margaret
trying to pull free of the robot, which was still blinking red
and grinding at the carpet. "Cooperate," squawked the robot. The man in the robe squinted at them, finally smiled.
"Please," said Margaret. "Fountain pens, eh?" the man in
the robe said at last. "Yes," said Margaret desperately,
and he heard himself add, "And beer—" "Yes, of course,"
mumbled the man in the robe. "How silly of me. Come
in." "Sir, for your safety—" "They're fine," said the man
to the robot. "I'm expecting them. Let them in." The robot released its grip. The man in the robe turned and shuffled inside. They followed him, all three of them, into
poorly lit rooms disastrously heaped with newspapers,
clothes, soiled dishes, empty and half-empty takeout packages, but still unmistakably the rooms from his tape, every
turn of his head recalling some camera movement and
there sure enough was the wall that had held the shadow,
the momentary stain of murder. The man in the robe
turned and said to the robot, "Please wait outside." "But
surely I should chaperone, sir—" "No, that's fine, just outside the door, I'll call you in if I need you. Close it on your
way out, thanks." Watching the robot slink back out he

couldn't help but feel a little thrill of vindication. The man in the robe continued into the kitchen, and gesturing at the table said, "Please, sit, sorry for the mess. Did you say you'd like a beer?" "Well, uh, no, that wasn't exactly—if you drink beer you ought to make it a Very Old Money Lager for full satisfaction—but I've got something else to discuss while you enjoy your delicious, oh, damn it—" "Relax, have a seat. Can I get you something else?" "Food," he blurted. "Which always goes best with a Very Old Money," and meanwhile Margaret released his hand and took a seat and started in talking about pens. The man opened his refrigerator, which was as overloaded as the apartment, another image from the tape now corrupted by squalor. "You poor people, stuck with those awful patches and yet I suppose I wouldn't have the benefit of your company today without them! Ah, well. Here, I wasn't expecting visitors but would you like some cheese? Can I fix you a glass of water?" The man set out a crumbled hunk of cheddar with a butter knife, crumbs on the dish and so long uncovered the edges were dried a deep, translucent orange. "So, you were just Advertising and you thought you'd pay a house call? How am I so lucky?" "Well, that's not it exactly—" Margaret took the knife and began paring away the edges of the cheese, carving out a chunk that looked more or less edible and when she handed it to him he couldn't resist, but tried talking through the mouthful anyway, desperately trying to negotiate the three priorities of hunger, Advertising, and his investigation: "Would you consider, mmmpphh, excuse me, consider opening a nice tall bottle of Very Old Money and settling in to watch this videotape I brought with me because there's something I'd like you to see, a question I've got about it—" The man in the robe nodded absently, half listening, staring oddly at Margaret and then said, "By all means let me see your tape—is it about beer? I'd be delighted but no hurry, please relax and enjoy yourselves, I'll be right out," and stepped into the living room, began rummaging among his possessions of which there certainly were plenty. It was a little depressing how full the once glorious apartment had gotten. Margaret cut him another piece of cheese and whispered, "Do you think he knows something?" "I can't know he seems so nice, well if not nice then harmless, hapless, but I'll judge his reaction to the video, watch him closely when the time comes—" grabbing more cheese quickly while he could and then the man in the robe was back. "Hello, friends, enjoying yourselves?" His robe had fallen open and they both stared but maybe it was just an example of his sloppiness. Certainly there was no polite way to mention it. There was something confusing about this man, who now went to the table and took the knife out of Margaret's hands and held her hand there for a moment and then snapped something—was it a bracelet?—around her wrist. Not a bracelet. Handcuffs. "Hey, wait a minute, that's no way to enjoy a nice glass of lager!" he heard himself say idiotically cheese falling out of his mouth jumping up as the man clicked Margaret's other wrist into the cuffs and he had her linked to the back of her chair. He stood to intervene

and the man in the robe swept his feet out from under him
with a kick and pushed him in the chest and he fell, feet
sliding on papers, hand skidding in lumps of cheese, to
the floor. "Thirsty!" he shouted, the more excited the
more fervent the Advertising, apparently. "No! Beer!" as
he struggled to get up. And Margaret was saying something desperate about Eiger fountain pens "—*self-refilling
cartridge*—" The man in the robe moved quickly, not lazy
and sloppy at all now and kicked away his satchel with the
tape inside and bent over him and reached behind his ear
to tear the patch away, another momentary sting. He could
only shout "Beer!" once more before the twilight world of
the One-Way Permeable Barrier surrounded him, it was
everywhere here, even Margaret was on the other side as
long as she wore the patch, and he felt his voice sucked
away to a scream audible inside the space of his own head
but not elsewhere, he knew, not until he was back outside,
on the street where he belonged and why couldn't he have
stayed there? What was he thinking? Anyway it wouldn't
be long now because through the gauze he saw the man in
the robe who you'd have to call the man half out of his
robe now open the door to let the robot in, then as the
naked man grinned at him steel pinchers clamped onto his
arm and he was dragged out of the room, screaming in-
audibly, thrashing to no purpose, leaving Margaret behind. And his tape besides.

The Spray

THE APARTMENT WAS BURGLED AND THE
police came. Four of them and a dog. The three youngest
were like boys. They wore buzzing squawking radios on
their belts. The oldest was in charge and the young ones
did what he told them. The dog sat. They asked what was
taken and we said we weren't sure—the television and the
fax machine, at least. One of them was writing, taking
down what we said. He had a tic, an eye that kept blinking. "What else?" the oldest policeman said. We didn't
know what else. That's when they brought it out, a small
unmarked canister, and began spraying around the house.
First they put a mask over the mouth and nose of the dog.

None of them wore a mask. They didn't offer us any protection. Just the dog. "Stand back," they said. They sprayed in a circle toward the edges of the room. We stood clustered with the policemen. "What's that?" we said. "Spray," said the oldest policeman. "Makes lost things visible."

The spray settled like a small rain through the house and afterward glowing in various spots were the things the burglar had taken. It was a salmon-colored glow. On the table was a salmon-colored image of a box, a jewelry box that Addie's mother had given us. There was a salmon-colored glowing television and fax machine in place of the missing ones. On the shelves the spray showed a Walkman and a camera and a pair of cuff links, salmon-colored and luminous. In the bedroom was Addie's vibrator, glowing like a fuel rod. We all walked around the apartment, looking for things. The eye-tic policeman wrote down the names of the items that appeared. Addie called the vibrator a massager. The dog in the mask, eyes watering. I couldn't smell the spray. "How long does it last?" we said.

"About a day," said the policeman who'd done the spraying, not the oldest. "You know you c-can't use this stuff anymore, even though you c-can see it," he said. "It's gone."

"Try and touch it," said the oldest policeman. He pointed at the glowing jewelry box.

We did and it wasn't there. Our hands passed through the visible missing objects.

They asked us about our neighbors. We told them we

trusted everyone in the building. They looked at the fire escape. The dog sneezed. They took some pictures. The burglars had come through the window. Addie put a book on the bedside table on top of the glowing vibrator. It showed through, like it was projected onto the book. We asked if they wanted to dust for fingerprints. The older policeman shook his head. "They wore gloves," he said. "How do you know?" we said. "Rubber gloves leave residue, powder," he said. "That's what makes the dog sneeze." "Oh." They took more pictures. "Did you want something to drink?" The older one said no. One of the younger policemen said, "I'm allergic, just like the d-dog," and the other policemen laughed. Addie had a drink, a martini. The policemen shook our hands and then they went away. We'd been given a case number. The box and the cuff links and the rest still glowed. Then Addie saw that the policemen had left the spray.

She took the canister and said, "There was something wrong with those policemen."

"Do you mean how young they seemed?"

"No, I think they always look young. You just don't notice on the street. Outdoors you see the uniforms, but in the house you can see how they're just barely old enough to vote."

"What are you going to do with that?" I said.

She handled it. "Nothing. Didn't you think there was something strange about those policemen, though?"

"Do you mean the one with the lisp?"

"He didn't have a lisp, he had a twitchy eye."

"Well, there was one with an eye thing, but the one who stuttered—is that what you mean by strange?" Addie kept turning the canister over in her hands. "Why don't you let me take that," I said.

"It's okay," she said. "I guess I don't know what I mean. Just something about them. Maybe there were too many of them. Do you think they develop the pictures themselves, Aaron? Do they have a darkroom in the police station?"

I said, "Probably." She said, "Do you think the missing things show up in the photographs—the things the spray reveals?"

"Probably."

"Let's just keep it and see if they come back."

"I wish you would put it on the table, then."

"Let's find a place to hide it."

"They're probably doing some kind of inventory right now, at the police station. They'll probably be back for it any minute."

"So if we hide it—"

"If we hide it we look guiltier than if you just put it on the table."

"We didn't steal anything. Our house was broken into. They left it here."

"I wish you would put it on the table."

"I wonder if the police do their inventory by spraying around the police station to see what's missing?"

"So if we have their spray—"

"They'll never know what happened!" She shrieked with laughter. I laughed too. I moved next to her on the couch and we rolled and laughed like monkeys in a zoo. Still laughing, I put my hand on the spray canister. "Gimme," I said.

"Let go." Her laughter faded as she pulled at the can. The ends of several hairs were stuck to her tongue. I pulled on the can. And she pulled. We both pulled harder.

"Gimme," I said. I let go of the can and tickled her. "Gimme gimme gimme."

She grimaced and twisted away from me. "Not funny," she said.

"The police don't have their SPRAY!" I said, and kept tickling her.

"Not funny not funny." Slapping my hands away, she stood up.

"Okay. You're right, it's not funny. Put it on the table."

"Let's return it like you said."

"I'm too tired. Let's just hide it. We can return it tomorrow."

"Okay, I'll hide it. Cover your eyes."

"Not hide-and-seek. We have to agree on a place. A locked place."

"What's the big deal? Let's just leave it on the table." She put it on the table, beside the salmon-colored glowing box. "Maybe somebody will break in and take it. Maybe the police will break in."

"You're a little mixed up, I'd say." I moved closer to the table.

"I'm just tired." She pretended to yawn. "What a day."

"I don't miss the stuff that was taken," I said.

"You don't?"

"I hate television and faxes. I hate this little jewelry box."

"See if you're still saying that tomorrow, when you can't see them anymore."

"I only care about you, you, you." I grabbed the canister of spray. She grabbed it too. "Let go," she said.

"You're all I love, you're all that matters to me," I said.

We wrestled for the can again. We fell onto the couch together.

"Let's just put it down on the table," said Addie. "Okay." "Let go." "You first." "No, at the same time." We put it on the table.

"Are you thinking what I'm thinking," she said.

"I don't know, probably."

"What are you thinking?"

"What you're thinking."

"I'm not thinking anything."

"Then I'm not either."

"Liar."

"It probably doesn't work that way," I said. "The police wouldn't have a thing like that. It isn't the same thing."

"So why not try."

"Don't."

"You said it wouldn't work."

"Just don't. It's toxic. You saw them cover the dog's mouth."

"They didn't cover themselves. Anyway, I asked them about that when you were in the other room. They said it was so you wouldn't see the stuff the dog ate that fell out of its mouth. Because the dog is a very sloppy eater. So the spray would show what it had been eating recently, around the mouth. It's disgusting, they said."

"Now you're the liar."

"Let's just see."

I jumped up. "If you spray me I'll spray you," I shouted. The spray hit me as I moved across the room. The wet mist fell behind me, like a parachute collapsing in the spot where I'd been, but enough got on me. An image of Lucinda formed, glowing and salmon-colored.

Lucinda was naked. Her hair was short, like when we were together. Her head lay on my shoulder, her arms were around my neck, and her body was across my front. My shirt and jacket. Her breasts were mashed against me, but I couldn't feel them. Her knee was across my legs. I jumped backward but she came with me, radiant and insubstantial. I turned my head to see her face. Her expression was peaceful, but her little salmon-colored eyelids were half open.

"Ha!" said Addie. "I told you it would work."

"GIVE ME THAT!" I lunged for the spray. Addie ducked. I grabbed her arm and pulled her with me onto the couch. Me and Addie and Lucinda were all there together, Lucinda placidly naked. As Addie and I wrestled for the spray we plunged through Lucinda's glowing body, her luminous arms and legs.

I got my hands on the spray canister. We both had our hands on it. Four hands covering the one can. Then it went off. One of us pressed the nozzle, I don't know who. It wasn't Lucinda, anyway.

As the spray settled over us Charles became visible, poised over Addie. He was naked, like Lucinda. His glowing shoulders and legs and ass were covered with glowing salmon hair, like the halo around a lightbulb. His mouth was open. His face was blurred, like he was a picture someone had taken while he was moving his face, saying something.

"There you go," I said. "You got what you wanted." "I didn't want anything," said Addie.

We put the spray on the table.

"How long did the police say it would last?" I said. I tried not to look at Lucinda. She was right beside my head.

"About twenty-four hours. What time is it?"

"It's late. I'm tired. The police didn't say twenty-four hours. About a day, they said."

"That's twenty-four hours."

"Probably they meant it's gone the next day."

"I don't think so."

I looked at the television. I looked at the cuff links. I looked at Charles's ass. "Probably the sunlight makes it wear off," I said.

"Maybe."

"Probably you can't see it in the dark, in complete darkness. Let's go to bed."

We went into the bedroom. All four of us. I took off my shoes and socks. "Probably it's just attached to our clothes. If I take off my clothes and leave them in the other room—"

"Try it."

I took off my pants and jacket. Lucinda was attached to me, not the clothes. Her bare salmon knee was across my bare legs. I started to take off my shirt. Addie looked at me. Lucinda's face was on my bare shoulder.

"Put your clothes back on," said Addie.

I put them back on. Addie left her clothes on. We lay on top of the covers in our clothes. Lucinda and Charles were on top of us. I didn't know where to put my hands. I wondered how Addie felt about Charles's blurred face, his open mouth. I was glad Lucinda wasn't blurred. "Turn off the light," I said. "We won't be able to see them in the dark."

Addie turned off the light. The room was dark. Charles and Lucinda glowed salmon above us. Glowing in the blackness with the vibrator on the side table and the luminous dial of my watch.

"Just close your eyes," I said to Addie.

"You close yours first," she said.

Vivian Relf

PAPER LANTERNS WITH CANDLES INSIDE, their flames capering in imperceptible breezes, marked the steps of the walkway. Shadow and laughter spilled from the house above, while music shorn of all but its pulse made its way like ground fog across the eucalyptus-strewn lawn. Doran and Top and Evie and Miranda drifted up the stairs, into throngs smoking and kissing cheeks and elbowing one another on the porch and around the open front door. Doran saw the familiar girl there, just inside.

He squinted and smiled, to offer evidence he wasn't gawking. To convey what he felt: he recognized her. She blinked at him, and parted her mouth slightly, then nipped her lower lip. Top and Evie and Miranda pushed inside the kitchen, fighting their way to the drinks surely waiting on a counter or in the refrigerator, but Doran hung back. He pointed a finger at the familiar girl, and moved nearer to her. She turned from her friends.

The foyer was lit with strings of red plastic chili peppers. They drooped in waves from the molding, their glow blushing cheeks, foreheads, ears, teeth.

"I know you from somewhere," he said.

"I was just thinking the same thing."

"You one of Jorn's friends?"

"Jorn who?"

"Never mind," said Doran. "This is supposed to be Jorn's house, I thought. I don't know why I even mentioned it, since I don't know him. Or her."

"My friends brought me," said the girl. "I don't even know whose party this is. I don't know if *they* know."

"My friends brought me too," said Doran. "Wait, do you waitress at Elision, on Dunmarket?"

"I don't live here. I must know you from somewhere else."

"Definitely, you look really familiar."

They were yelling to be heard in the jostle of bodies inside the door. Doran gestured over their heads, outside. "Do you want to go where we can talk?"

They turned the corner, stopped in a glade just short of the deck, which was as full of revelers as the kitchen and foyer. They nestled in the darkness between pools of light and chatter. The girl had a drink, red wine in a plastic cup. Doran felt a little bare without anything.

"This'll drive me crazy until I figure it out," he said. "Where'd you go to college?"

"Sundstrom," she said.

"I went to Vagary." Doran swallowed the syllables, knowing it was a confession: *I'm one of those Vagary types*. "But I used to know a guy who went to Sundstrom. How old are you?"

"Twenty-six."

"I'm twenty-eight. You would have been there at the same time." This was hardly a promising avenue. But he persisted. "Gilly Noman, that ring a bell?"

"Sounds like a girl's name."

"I know, never mind. Where do you live?"

She mentioned a city, a place he'd never been.

"That's no help. How long have you lived there?"

"Since college. Five years, I guess."

"Where'd you grow up?"

The city she mentioned was another cipher, a destination never remotely considered.

"Your whole life?" he asked. Doran racked his brain, but he didn't know anyone from the place.

"Yeah," she said, a bit defensively. "What about you?"

"Right here, right around here. Wait, this is ridiculous. You look so familiar."

"So do you." She didn't sound too discouraged.

"Who are your friends here?"

"Ben and Malorie. You know them?"

"No, but do you maybe visit them often?"

"First time."

"You didn't, uh, go to Camp Drewsmore, did you?" Doran watched how his feelings about the girl changed, like light through a turned prism, as he tried to fit his bodily certainty of her familiarity into each proposed context. Summer camp, for instance, forced him to consider whether she'd witnessed ball-field humiliations, or kissed one of the older boys who were his idol then, he, in his innocence, not having yet kissed anyone.

"No."

"Drewsmore-in-the-Mist?"

"Didn't go to camp."

"Okay, wait, forget camp, it must be something more recent. What do you do?"

"Until just now I worked on Congressman Goshen's campaign. We, uh, lost. So I'm sort of between things. What do you do?"

"Totally unrelated in every way. I'm an artist's assistant. Heard of London Jerkins?"

"No."

"To describe it briefly there's this bright purple zigzag in all his paintings, kind of a signature shape. I paint it." He mimed the movements, the flourish at the end. "By now I do it better than him. You travel a lot for the congressman thing?"

"Not ever. I basically designed his pamphlets and door hangers."

"Ah, our jobs aren't so different after all."

"But I don't have one now." She aped his zigzag flourish, as punctuation.

"Hence you're crashing parties in distant cities which happen to be where I live."

"Hey, you didn't even know if Jorn was a guy or a girl. I at least was introduced, though I didn't catch his name."

He put up his hands: no slight intended. "But where do I know you from? I mean, no pressure, but this is mutual, right? You recognize me too."

"I was sure when you walked in. Now I'm not so sure."

"Yeah, maybe you look a little less familiar yourself."

In the grade of woods over the girl's shoulder Doran sighted two pale copper orbs, flat as coins. Fox? Bunny? Raccoon? He motioned for the girl to turn and see, when at that moment Top approached them from around the corner of the house. Doran's hand fell, words died on his lips. Tiny hands or feet scrabbled urgently in the underbrush, as though they were repairing a watch. The noise vanished.

Top had his own cup of wine, half empty. Lipstick smudged his cheek. Doran moved to wipe it off, but Top bobbed, ducking Doran's reach. He glared. "Where'd you go?" he asked Doran, only nodding his chin at the familiar girl.

"We were trying to figure out where we knew each other from," said Doran. "This is my friend Top. I'm sorry, what's your name?"

"Vivian."

"Vivian, Top. And I'm Doran."

"Hello, Vivian," said Top, curtly, raising his cup. To Do-ran: "You coming inside?"

"Sure, in a minute."

Top raised his eyebrows, said: "Sure. Anyway, we'll be there. Me and Evie and Miranda." To Vivian: "Nice to meet you." He slipped around the corner again.

"Friends waiting for you?" said Vivian.

"Sure, I guess. Yours?"

"It's not the same. They're a couple."

"Letting you mingle, I guess that's what you mean."

"Whereas yours are what—dates?"

"Good question. It's unclear, though. I'd have to admit they're maybe dates. But only maybe. Vivian what?"

"Relf."

"Vivian Relf. Totally unfamiliar. I'm Doran Close. In case that triggers any recall." Doran felt irritable, reluc-tant to let go of it, possibly humiliated, in need of a drink.

"It doesn't."

"Have we pretty much eliminated everything?"

"I can't think of anything else."

"We've never been in any of the same cities or schools or anything at the same time." It gave him a queasy, earth-shifty sensation. As though he'd come through the door of the party wrong, on the wrong foot. Planted a foot or flag on the wrong planet: one small step from the foyer, one gi-ant plunge into the abyss.

"Nope, I don't think so."

"You're not on television?"

"Never."

"So what's the basis of all this howling familiarity?"

"I don't know if there really is any basis, and anyway I'm not feeling such howling familiarity anymore."

"Right, me neither." This was now a matter of pure vertigo, cliff-side terror. He didn't hold it against Vivian Relf, though. She was his fellow sufferer. It was what they had in common, the sole thing.

"You want to go back to your friends?" she said.

"I guess so."

"Don't feel bad."

"I don't," lied Doran.

"Maybe I'll see you around."

"Very good then, Less-Than-Familiar-Girl. I'll look forward to that." Doran offered his hand to shake, mock-pompously. He felt garbed in awkwardness.

Vivian Relf accepted his hand, and they shook. She'd grown a little sulky herself, at the last minute.

Doran found Top and Evie and Miranda beyond the kitchen, in a room darkened and lit only by a string of Christmas lights, and cleared of all but two enormous speakers, as though for dancing. No one danced, no one inhabited the room apart from the three of them. There was something petulant in choosing to shout over the music, as they were doing.

"Who's your new friend?" said Miranda.

"Nobody. I thought she was an old friend, actually."

"Sure you weren't just attracted to her?"

"No, it was a shock of recognition, of seeing someone

completely familiar. The weird thing is she had the same thing with me, I think." The language available to Doran for describing his cataclysm was cloddish and dead, the words a sequence of corpses laid head to toe.

"Yeah, it's always mutual."

"What's that supposed to mean?"

"Nothing, nothing."

"Look around this party," said Doran. "How many people could you say you've never been in a room together with before? That they didn't actually attend a lower grade in your high school, that you couldn't trace a link to their lives? That's what she and I just did. We're perfect strangers."

"Maybe you saw her on an airplane."

Doran had no answer for this. He fell silent.

Later that night he saw her again, across two rooms, through a doorway. The party had grown. She was talking to someone new, a man, not her friends. He felt he still recognized her, but the sensation hung uselessly in a middle distance, suspended, as in amber, in doubt so thick it was a form of certainty. She irked him, that was all he knew.

• • •

IT WAS two years before he saw the familiar girl again, at another party, again in the hills. They recognized one another immediately.

"I know you," she said, brightening.

"Yes, I know you too, but from where?" The moment he

said it he recalled their conversation. "Of course, how could I forget? You're that girl *I don't know*."

"Oh, yeah." She seemed to grow immensely sad.

They stood together contemplating the privileges of their special relationship, its utter and proven vacancy.

"It's like when you start a book and then you realize you read it before," he said. "You can't really remember anything ahead, only you know each line as it comes to you."

"No surprises to be found, you mean?" She pointed at herself.

"Just a weird kind of pre—" He searched for the word he meant. Pre*formatting*? Pre*cognition*? Pre-*exhaustion*?

"More like a stopped car on the highway slowing down traffic," she said, seemingly uninterested in his ending the unfinished word. "Not a gaudy crash or anything. Just a cop waving you along, saying *Nothing to see here*."

"Doran," he said.

"Vivian."

"I remember. You visiting your friends again?"

"Yup. And before you ask I have no idea whose party this is or what I'm doing here."

"Probably you were looking for me."

"I've got a boyfriend," she said. The line that was always awkward, in anyone's language. Then, before he could respond, she added: "I'm only joking."

"Oh."

"Just didn't want you thinking of me as Ben and Malorie's, oh, sort of *party accessory*. The extra girl, the floater."

"No, never the extra girl. The girl I don't know from anywhere, that's you."

"Funny to meet the girl you don't know, twice," she said. "When there are probably literally thousands of people you do know or anyway could establish a connection with who you never even meet once."

"I'm tempted to say small world."

"Either that or we're very large people."

"But maybe we're evidence of the opposite, I'm thinking now. Large *world*."

"We're not evidence of anything," said Vivian Relf. She shook his hand again. "Enjoy the party."

•   •   •

THE NEXT time *was* on an airplane, a coast-to-coast flight. Doran sat in first class. Vivian Relf trundled past him, headed deep into the tail, carry-on hugged to her chest. She didn't spot him.

He mused on sending back champagne with the stewardess, as in a cocktail lounge—*From the man in 3A.* There was probably a really solid reason they didn't allow that. A hundred solid reasons. He didn't dwell on Vivian Relf, watched a movie instead. Barbarian hordes were vanquished in waves of slaughter, twenty thousand feet above the plain.

They spoke at the baggage carousel. She didn't seem overly surprised to see him there.

"As unrelated baggage mysteriously commingles in the

dark belly of an airplane only to be redistributed to its proper possessor in the glare of daylight on the whirring metal belt, so you repeatedly graze my awareness in shunting through the dimmed portals of my life," he said. "Doran Close."

"Vivian Relf," she said, shaking his hand. "But I suspect you knew that."

"Then you've gathered that I'm obsessed with you."

"No, it's that nobody ever forgets my name. It's one of those that sticks in your head."

"Ah."

She stared at him oddly, waiting. He spotted, beneath her sleeve, the unmistakable laminated wristlet of a hospital stay, imprinted RELF, VIVIAN, RM 315.

"I'd propose we share a cab but friends are waiting to pick me up in the white zone." He jerked his thumb at the curb.

"The odds are we're anyway pointed in incompatible directions."

"Ah, if I've learned anything at all in this life it's not to monkey with the odds."

There was a commotion. Some sort of clog at the mouth where baggage was disgorged. An impatient commuter clambered up to straddle the chugging belt. He rolled up suit sleeves and tugged the jammed suitcases out of the chute. The backlog tumbled loose, a miniature avalanche. Doran's suitcase was among those freed. Vivian Relf still waited, peering into the hole as though at a distant horizon. Doran, feeling giddy, left her there.

All that week, between appointments with art collec-
tors and gallerists, he spied for her in the museums and
bistros of the vast metropolis, plagued by the ghost of certainty they'd come here, to this far place, this neutral site,
apart but together, in order to forge some long-delayed
truce or compact. The shrouded visages of the locals
formed a kind of brick wall, an edifice which met his gaze
everywhere: forehead, eyebrows, glasses, grim-drawn lips,
cell phones, sandwiches. Against this background she'd
have blazed like a sun. But never appeared.

· · ·

Oh Vivian Relf! Oh eclipse, oh pale penumbra of my
    yearning!
Pink slip, eviction notice, deleted icon, oh!
Stalked in alleys of my absent noons, there's nobody
knows you better than I!
Translucent voracious Relf-self, I vow here
Never again once to murk you
With pallid tropes of familiarity *or* recognition
You, pure apparition, onion—
Veil of veils only!

· · ·

DORAN CLOSE, in his capacity as director of acquisitions
in drawings and prints, had several times had lunch with

Vander Polymus, the editor of *Wall Art*. He'd heard Polymus mention that he, Polymus, was married. He'd never met the man's wife, though, and it was a surprise, as he stepped across Polymus's threshold for the dinner party, bottle of Cabernet Franc in a scarf of tissue thrust forward in greeting, to discover that the amiable ogre was married to someone he recognized. Not from some previous museum fete or gallery opening but from another life, another frame of reference, years before. Really, from another postulated version of his life, his sense, once, of who he'd be. He knew her despite the boyishly short haircut, the jarring slash of lipstick and bruises of eyeshadow, the freight of silver bracelets: Vander Polymus was married to Vivian Relf.

Meeting her eyes, Doran unconsciously reached up and brushed his fingertips to his shaved skull.

"Doran, Viv," said Polymus, grabbing Doran by the shoulder and tugging him inside. "Throw your coat on the bed. I'll take that. C'mon. Hope you like pernil and bacalao!"

"Hello," she said, and as Doran relinquished the bottle she took his hand to shake.

"Vivian Relf," said Doran.

"Vivian Polymus," she confirmed.

"Shall we pry open your bottle?" said Vander Polymus. "Is it something special? I've got a Rioja I'm itching to sample. You know each other?"

"We met, once," said Vivian. "Other side of the world."

Doran wanted to emend her *once*, but couldn't find his voice.

"Did you fucking fuck my wife?" chortled Polymus, fingers combing his beard. "You'll have to tell me all about it, but save it for dinner. There's people I want you to meet."

So came the accustomed hurdles: the bottles opened and appreciated; the little dinner-party geometries: *No, but of course I know your name* or *If I'm not wrong your gallery represents my dear friend Zeus*; the hard and runny cheeses and the bowl of aggravatingly addictive salted nuts; the dawning apprehension that a single woman in the party of eight had been tipped his way by the scheming Polymus and another couple, who'd brought her along—much as, so long ago, Vivian Relf had been shopped at parties by the couple she'd been visiting. Hurdles? Really these were placed low as croquet wickets. Yet they had to be negotiated for a time, deftly, with a smile, before Doran could at last find himself seated. Beside the single woman, of course, but gratefully, as well, across from Polymus's wife. Vivian Relf.

He raised his glass to her, slightly, wishing to draw her nearer, wishing they could tip their heads together for murmuring.

"I used to think I'd keep running into you forever," he said.

She only smiled. Her husband intruded from the end of the table, his voice commanding. "What is it with you two?" Irrationally, Polymus's own impatience seemed

to encompass the years since Doran and Vivian's first
meeting, the otherwise forgettable, and forgotten, party.
Doran wondered if anyone else on the planet had reason
to recall that vanished archipelago of fume, conversation,
and disco, tonight or ever. The ancient party was like a radio signal dopplering through outer space, it seemed to
him now.

"You fuck him, Viv?" said Polymus. "Inquiring minds
want to know."

"No," said Vivian Relf-Polymus. "No, but we were
probably flirting. This was a long time ago."

Polymus and his wife had captured the attention of the
whole table, with evident mutual pleasure.

"We had this funny thing," Doran felt compelled to explain. "You remember? We didn't know anyone in common. You seemed really familiar, but we'd never met
before."

This drew a handful of polite laughs, cued principally
by the word *funny*, and perhaps by Doran's jocular tone.
Beneath it he felt desperate. Vander Polymus only scowled,
as for comic effect he might scowl at an awkwardly hung
painting, or at a critical notice with which he violently dis-
agreed.

"What I remember is you had these awful friends," said
Vivian. "They didn't hesitate to show they found me a
poor way for you to be spending your time. What was that
tall moody boy's name?"

"Top," said Doran, only remembering as he blurted it.

He hadn't thought of Top for years, had in fact forgotten
Top was present at the Vivian Relf Party.

"Were you breaking up with some girl that night?"

"No," said Doran. "Nothing like that." He couldn't remember.

"If looks could kill."

Those people mean nothing to me, Doran wished to
cry. *They barely did at the time. And now, what was it,
ten years later?* It was Vivian Relf who mattered, couldn't
she see?

"Do you remember the airport?" he asked.

"Ah, the *airport*," said Polymus, with a connoisseur's
sarcasm. "Now we're getting somewhere. Tell us about the
airport."

The table chuckled nervously, all in deference to their
host.

"I haven't the faintest idea what he's talking about, my
love."

"It's nothing," said Doran. "I saw you, ah, at an airport
once." He suddenly wished to diminish it, in present company. He saw now that something precious was being
taken from him in full view, a treasure he'd found in his
possession only at the instant it was squandered. *I wrote a
poem to you once, Vivian Relf*, he said silently, behind a
sip of excellent Rioja. Doran knew it was finer, much more
interesting, than the wine he'd brought, the Cabernet
Franc they'd sipped with their appetizers.

He might have known Vivian Relf better than anyone he
actually knew, Doran thought now. Or anyway, he'd

wanted to. It ought to mean the same thing. His soul creaked in irrelevant despair.

"This is boring," pronounced Vander Polymus.

The dinner party rose up and swallowed them, as it was meant to.

Planet Big Zero

MY HOUSE IS PROTECTED FROM THE STREET by a wooden fence six feet high, so solidly built that it's practically a wall. You can't look through it. The fence gate swings open smoothly, an inch from the paved walkway, without sticking or wobbling. Returning home a few days ago, I stepped up and pushed the gate open, as I always do, without breaking my stride. This day the gate bumped hard against something on the other side.

Annoyed, I pushed harder, and stepped through the space I'd wedged open. Lying on the walkway, rubbing his head, was a bum. I'd whacked him on the top of his skull with the gate. After a confused moment I grasped the situation: he'd ducked in from the street, then stretched out to warm in the sun in the first place he found. I live next door to a supermarket. He was probably napping after a meal of salvage from the dumpster in the alley. I knew that bums sometimes slept the night in the alley, though they always kept out of sight.

He wasn't knocked out. He made a sort of rasping, moaning sound and rolled onto his side.

Then we had the strangest conversation.

"You okay?" I said, defensively gruff.

"Yeah," he said. He was bald on top, so I could see that there wasn't a gash.

"That's a hell of a place to be," I said, justifying myself.

He said something I couldn't quite make out. It sounded like, "Every place has its price."

"What?"

"That's the price of this place." Or something. I was already walking away, toward my door. I'd seen that he was both unharmed and harmless.

"Well, take care of yourself," I said.

"Don't worry about me," he said.

Then I went inside, and for the briefest moment, tried to think about what had happened. *I just hit a man in the head with a big piece of wood,* I told myself. A part of me insisted that it was a notable event, something disturbing, something extreme. I'd certainly never done anything like it before.

But that part of me lost out. My attention just slid away. I literally *couldn't* keep my mind on it.

I mention this because of the light it sheds on what happened with Matthew.

•   •   •

WHEN MATTHEW and I were in high school we had a running joke that I think epitomized our sense of humor. Our school featured special programs for musically talented students. For that reason, or for no reason at all, there was a bust of Toscanini in the middle of the main hall of the building. It was a dingy bronze, slightly larger than life-size. Toscanini gazed out with a stolid, heroic air, his thick oxidized hair flowing back in the sculptor's imaginary breeze. He could have been a general, or a football coach, but a plaque on the pillar informed us that it was in fact Toscanini. It was typical of Matthew and me that we even noticed the sculpture. I doubt if any of the other students could have confirmed its existence if we'd mentioned it to them. We never did.

The joke was exclusively between us and some unseen janitor or security guard. Every week or so for a whole term, on our way out of the building after our last class, Matthew and I would hurriedly tape a pair of eyeglass frames, crudely fashioned from torn notebook paper and scotch tape, across Toscanini's glaring eyes. The glasses were never there when we returned in the morning. They were probably torn away within minutes, but that didn't matter to us. The sight of the paper glasses on the bronze was funny, but only initially was it the point of the joke.

The real point was saying it, again and again. "Toscanini's glasses." As though those glasses were a landmark, the one certainty in an uncertain universe. Whatever subject was at hand, the glasses were the comparison we'd reach for first. "What didn't you understand? It was as clear as Toscanini's glasses." Or "Cool, man, like Toscanini's glasses." Or "No more urgent than, say, Toscanini's glasses." If one of us forgot what he was going to say, the other would gently suggest, "Something about Toscanini's glasses?"

It was a joke about futility, and at the same time a joke about will, and subjectivity. If we filibustered the glasses into existence between us did it matter that the paper-and-tape glasses didn't persist? Worlds seemed to hang in the balance of that unspoken question, and in a way they did. Our worlds. The glasses stood for our own paper-thin new sensibilities, thrust against the bronze of the adult world. Were we viable? Did we have to convince others, or was it enough just to convince ourselves?

The question was made immediate by our careers as students. Did it matter that you were smarter than your English teacher if she could fail you for cutting class to smoke pot in the park? Matthew and I gave her that chance, and she took it. When college-application time rolled around, the costs were suddenly apparent. You couldn't get into an Ivy League school on the strength of private jokes.

Actually, I did. For the essay section of my Yale application I drew a ten-page comic, of the soul-searching,

R. Crumb variety. It took me three weeks, and it was by far the most sustained effort I'd made in the four years of high school, or in my life to that point. I remember Matthew calling me at home during those weeks, wanting to know what was wrong. I couldn't explain.

The comic led to an unusual interview with a Yale scout. The first question he asked was what my favorite single book was. I said *Travels in Arabia Deserta*, which I'd never read. He looked taken aback. "That's *my* favorite book," he said. "I didn't realize anyone your age was reading it." "Yeah, well," I said. "I'm an autodidact." I hoped that would account for my grades. I don't know if it did, but I had the scout eating out of my hand after the lucky coincidence. Fortunately he didn't ask me what I liked about *Arabia Deserta*.

Matthew got into Reed. I helped him get the application out, in one desperate night before the deadline. Reed is one of those colleges where they don't give grades, where you can major in things like harmonica or earth sculpture. It's in the Pacific Northwest, far from New York, which probably would have been good for him. But he didn't go. He convinced his parents that he needed a year abroad before he could decide what to do. Sending him to college would have cost about the same, so they went for it. He and his marijuana fumes were out of the house either way.

Matthew was talking about becoming a Zen monk a lot at that time, and he even carried around an Alan Watts book called *The Wisdom of Insecurity* for a while. I'm sure he thought our pranks were a form of native Zen. An example: We took an 8-by-11 sheet of clear Mylar to the Xerox shop and asked for a copy. The clerk indulged us. The result was a photograph of the inside of the machine, of course, but Matthew insisted on calling it "a copy of nothing." Just like one hand clapping, see? He cared nothing about Buddhism, needless to say. If there had been such a thing as a Dada monk he would have wanted to become that. But Zen it was, so he went to Asia.

Matthew visited me once at Yale, junior year. I lived in a suite with a roommate, and I was embarrassed to have Matthew stay there. He and I were beginning to look different. He was sunburned and wiry and seemed quite a bit older. He was still dressed like a boy but he looked like a man. At Yale we all dressed like men but looked like boys, except for a few who were working on beer stomachs.

Matthew was back temporarily from Thailand, where, he explained excitedly, he'd gotten involved with a charismatic drug lord named Khan Shah. Khan Shah was more powerful than the government, Matthew said, and was trying to legitimize his rule by making poppy cultivation legal. He was a man of the people. Matthew was learning to speak Thai so he could translate Khan Shah's manifestos.

This didn't sound like Zen to me, and I told Matthew so. He laughed.

"Are you doing what you want to do?" he asked me suddenly.

That question didn't compute for me at the time.

Matthew was making me very, very nervous. I could still admire him, but I didn't want him in my life.

Cracking old jokes for cover, I hustled him back down to New York with excuses about a girlfriend's demands and a paper I had to write. He spent just one night.

That was the last I saw of him for eight years. Except for postcards. Here's one from a few years back. The front shows Elton John, in spangled glasses. In Matthew's hand on the back it says "Vacant Lot/Living Chemist." No return address. The postmark is Santa Fe, New Mexico.

● ● ●

I ONLY had an hour's warning. He got my number from information, he explained on the phone. I gave him the address. An hour later he knocked on my door.

He wobbled slightly. "I parked in the green zone," he said.

"That's fine, it's two hours." I stared. He was still tall and bony, but his face was fleshy and red. I immediately wondered if I looked as bad, if I'd lost as much.

"Here," he said. "I brought you this."

It was a rock, fist-sized, gray with veins of white. I took it.

"Thanks," I said, checking the irony in my voice. I didn't know whether I was supposed to think it was mainly funny or mainly profound that he'd brought me a rock.

If it was high school there would have been a punch

line. He would have led me out to the curb to see the trunk-load of identical rocks in his car.

Ten years later, that kind of follow-through was gone. Matthew's gestures were shrouded and gnomic. Trees falling in forests.

"Come in," I said.

"I saw the Piggly Wiggly when I parked," he said. "I thought I'd get some beer."

It was two in the afternoon. "Okay," I said.

A few minutes later he was back in the doorway with a rustling paper bag. He unloaded a six-pack of Sierra Nevada into my fridge and opened a tall aluminum canister of Japanese beer to drink right away. We poured it into two glasses. I wrote off getting anything accomplished that afternoon.

He leaned back and smiled at me, but his eyes were nervous. "Nice place," he said.

"It's a place where I can get work done," I said, feeling weirdly defensive.

"I see your stuff whenever I can," he said earnestly. "My parents clip them for me."

I draw a one-page comic called *Planet Big Zero*, for a free music magazine produced by a record-store chain. Once a month my characters, Dr. Fahrenheit and Sniveling Toon (and their little dog, Louie Louie), have a stupid adventure and review a new CD by a major rock act.

Somewhere in there you might detect the dying heartbeat of Toscanini's glasses. It's a living, anyway. Better than a living recently, since a cable video channel bought rights to develop *Planet* into a weekly animated feature, and hired me to do scripts and storyboards.

"I didn't realize your folks were into rock journalism," I said.

"My parents are really proud of you," Matthew said, working diligently on his beer. He wasn't being sarcastic. There was nothing challenging left in his persona, except what I projected.

He told me his story. Since Santa Fe he'd been in Peru, taking pictures of plinths and other ancient structures. He talked a lot about "sites." The term covered a sculpture in Texas made of upended Cadillacs half buried in the desert, stone rings in Tibet, a circular graveyard in Paris, and Wall Street skyscrapers. He'd shot hundreds of rolls of film. None of it was developed. He was trying to get funding to create a CD-ROM. In the tales he told there were ghosts, mostly women, scurrying out of the frame. An expatriate Englishwoman he'd lived with in Mexico City who'd thrown him out. A female journalist who'd been his collaborator, then disappeared with his only photos of an Inca burial site that had since been destroyed. And the bitch in the Florida Keys just now who'd stolen his camera after a shared three-day drunk.

I live in Connecticut, an hour out of the city if there's no traffic. Matthew had driven up to see me in his parents' car. He was in New York trying to convince his parents to cash out ten thousand dollars in zero coupon bonds they were holding in his name, presumably for when he married and bought a house. He was willing to take a hit on early-withdrawal penalties, so that he could use what remained to fund his return to Peru.

He'd become some combination of an artist with the temperament, but no art, and Thor Heyerdahl without a raft.

The Japanese canister was empty. Matthew went into the kitchen for the first of the Sierras, unapologetically. He wasn't drinking like he was on a tear, or wanted to be. It was as though the beer was a practical necessity, like he needed it for ballast.

"If you don't want to drive back down tonight you can stay in the garage," I told him. "It's set up as a guest room. You can pee in the sink in there. I'll give you a key to the house so you can shower or whatever."

"That's great," he said. His look was humble and piercing, both. "You know, it's really amazing to see you again."

I sort of flinched. "The same," I said.

"It's amazing how little has changed after all this time."

I wasn't aware of that being the case, in any sense at all. But I nodded.

That night we got on a roll in safe territory, talking about high school. The Water Fountain Trick. The Literary Excuse Me. Mother Communication Hates You. Falling Down Jesus Park. Toscanini's Glasses. Then, fueled by beer, I told him a bit about my life, my short marriage, the novel I couldn't sell, the years of legal proofreading. Matthew drank and listened. He listened well.

Then he started telling me about his idea for a screen-play we were going to write together. "Has there ever been a thriller set in Antarctica?" he asked, eyes burning.

"*Ice Station Zebra*," I said. "Rock Hudson's in it. It's really bad. Listen, I'm bushed."

He slept in. I was working at my desk for hours before I heard him go in through the kitchen, up to the bathroom for a shower. The water ran for almost twenty minutes. I'm not sure, but I think he must have come out while I was on the phone with my Hollywood agent.

As I get older I find that the friendships that are the most certain, ultimately, are the ones where you and the other person have made substantial amounts of money for one another. Those histories have a breadth, an unspoken ease, that others, even siblings or ex-wives, just can't match. My Hollywood agent is about my age, and when I talk to him I feel he knows who I am, because he helped make me who I am. We're a conspiracy, and a much more reliable one than most.

Some time after I'd hung up the phone, I became aware of Matthew standing in the doorway of my office. "Did you hear me talking to you?" he said.

"Uh, no."

His eyes were ringed and dark. He didn't speak.

"There's coffee in the kitchen," I said. "It's still hot."

When he returned with the coffee he came all the way into the room and stood in front of me. He seemed dis-concerted.

"I think I'll go check out that old foundry today," he

said. "There's some wrecked equipment I always wanted
to take pictures of."

"No camera," I reminded him.

"Well, I guess I'll just go look at it."

Ruins, I thought. Wrecks, shambles, margins. Zen junk.

"That's fine, I'll be here," I said. "I have some stuff to
do. We can go out for dinner tonight."

"We could cook something," he began. I could see him
grasping, trying to frame some larger question.

"I'd like to take you out," I said—magnanimity being
one of the most effective ways of ending conversations. I
was thinking of my work. I had to get back to harnessing
our high-school sensibility to the task of selling compact
discs.

• • •

HE WAS back at five, with another bag from the Piggly
Wiggly. Inside was a full six-pack, and another one full of
empties. He'd been out all day looking at sites and drinking beer from a paper bag. He put the empties on the
porch and the six in the fridge, like an obedient dog moving slippers to the bedroom.

I'd arranged for us to meet a couple of friends for dinner.
A science-fiction writer who does scenarios for interactive
video games, and a screenwriter. We all have the same Hollywood agent, which is how we met. I figured the screenwriter could sober Matthew up about his script ideas. I
didn't want to eat dinner with Matthew alone anyway.

We met for drinks first. By the time we got to the restaurant Matthew was lagging behind, already so invisible that the maître d' said, "Table for three?"

He barely spoke during dinner. At the end of the night we parted at my driveway, me to my front door, Matthew to the garage.

"Well, good night," I said.

He stopped. "You know, I realize I don't have everything quite together," he said.

"You've got a lot of interesting projects going," I said.

"I'm not asking you for anything." He glared, just briefly.

"Of course not."

"I feel strange around you," he said. "I can't explain." He looked at his hands, held them up against the light of the moon.

"You're just getting used to the way I am now," I said. "I've changed."

"No, it's me," he said.

"Get some sleep," I said.

I didn't see him in the morning, just heard the shower running, and the door to the refrigerator opening and closing.

•　•　•

ABOUT A week later, I hit on the idea of putting Matthew into *Planet Big Zero* as a character. It was a way of assuaging my own guilt, and of compartmentalizing the experience of seeing him again. I guess I also wanted to establish the connection between our old wide-open, searching form of humor and my current smug, essentially closed form.

As I drew Matthew into the panels it occurred to me that I was casting him into a prison by publishing him in the cartoon. Then I realized how silly that was. If he was in a prison he was there already, and the cartoon had nothing to do with it. He'd be delighted to see himself. I imagined showing it to him. Then I realized I wouldn't. Anyway, I finished the cartoon, and FedExed it to my editor.

Who hated it. "What's that guy doing there?" he said on the phone.

"He's a new character," I said.

"He's not funny," said the editor. "Can you take him out?"

"You want me to take him out?"

"He's not intrinsic to any of the scenes," said my editor. "He's just standing around."

• • •

THAT WAS two months ago. The point is, it wasn't until just the other day, when I hit the sleeping bum on the head with the gate, that I really gave any thought to the way things turned out. So much of what we do is automatic, so much of life becomes invisible. For instance, I've been buying six-packs and putting them in the fridge, but it isn't me drinking them. The empties pile up on the porch. I always forget to bring them out to the curb on recycling day. Sometimes the bums prowl around for bottles and do my work for me. I think somebody somewhere gives them a nickel apiece for them—another invisible operation, among so many.

Matthew's parents' car got towed after two weeks. It must have had ten or fifteen tickets pinned under the wiper. The authorities are pretty vigilant about that around here. As for Matthew, he's still in the garage. But he's been rendered completely transparent, unless, I suppose, you happen to be wearing Toscanini's glasses.

The Glasses

ROWS OF FRAMES SAT ON GLASS SHELVES, clear lenses reflecting gray light from the Brooklyn avenue. Outside, rain fell. At the door a cardboard box waited for umbrellas. The carpet was pink and yellow, to the limits of the floor, to the tightly seamed glass cases. The empty shop was like a cartoonist's eyeball workshop, hundreds of bare outlines yearning for pupils, for voices. They fell short of expression themselves. The whole shop fell short. There was no radio. The white-coated opticians leaned on their glass counters, dreaming of their wives, of beautiful women who needed glasses. One of them moved into the rear of the shop and made a call.

The other turned as the door chimed, two notes blurred momentarily in the rain's hiss.

"You're back."

"Damn fucking right I'm back." The black man wiped his feet just inside the door, though there wasn't a mat, then jogged forward into the shop. He wore a baseball cap, and his glasses.

The optician didn't move. "You don't need to use language," he said.

They'd sold him his glasses yesterday. One hundred dollars. He'd paid with cash, not out of a wallet.

The customer bounced from one foot to the other like a boxer. An ingrown beard scarred the underside of his long jaw. He pushed his chin forward, keeping his hands by his side. "Look. Same damn thing."

The optician grunted slightly and moved to look. He was as tall as the customer, and fatter. "A smudge," he said.

He was still purring in his boredom. This distraction hadn't persuaded him yet that it would become an event, a real dent in the afternoon.

"*Scratched*," said the customer. "Same as the last pair. If you can't fix the problem why'd you sell me the damn glasses?"

"A smudge," said the optician. "Clean it off. Here."

The customer ducked backward. "Keep off. Don't fool with me. Can't clean it off. They're already messed up. Like the old ones. They're *all messed up*."

"Let me see," said the optician.

"Where's Dr. Bucket? I want to talk to the doctor."

"*Burkhardt*. And he's not a doctor. Let me see." The optician drew in his stomach, adjusted his own glasses.

"*You're* not the doctor, man." The customer danced away recklessly, still thrusting out his chin.

"We're both the same," said the optician wearily. "We make glasses. Let me see."

The second optician came out of the back, smoothed his hair, and said, "What?"

"Bucket!"

The second optician looked at the first, then turned to the customer. "Something wrong with the glasses?"

"Same thing as yesterday. Same place. Look." Checking his agitation, he stripped his glasses off with his right hand and offered them to the second optician.

"First of all, you should take them off with two hands, like I showed you," said the second optician. He pinched the glasses at the two hinges, demonstrating. Then he turned them and raised them to his own face.

The inside of the lenses were marked, low and close to the nose.

"You touched them. That's the problem."

"No."

"Of course you did. That's fingerprints."

"Damn, Bucket, man. I'll show you the old ones. You can't even fix the problem."

"The problem is you touched them. Here." The second

optician went to the counter and dipped the glasses in a
shallow bath of cleanser, dried them with a chamois cloth.
The customer bobbed forward anxiously, trying to see.

"What do you, scratch at your eyes all the time?" said
the first optician, smiling now. The problem was solved.

"Shut up," said the customer, pointing a finger at the
first optician. "Just shut up. You're not my doctor on this."

"Nobody is," said the first optician. "You don't need a
doctor, you need to keep your hands out of your eyes."

"Shut up."

The second optician glared at the first. He handed the
glasses to the customer. "Let me see you put them on."

The customer bent his head down and lifted the glasses
to his face.

"Wait a minute, I couldn't see . . ."

"It's the *fit*."

"The bill of your cap was in the way," said the first optician.

"Put them on again," said the second.

"Same thing," said the customer, shaking his head. He
pulled off the glasses, again with one hand. "Look. Still
there. Little scratches."

The first optician stepped up close to the customer.
"Sure. You touched it again. When I couldn't see. It's how
you put them on."

"He uses his thumbs," said the second, snorting.

"Little scratches, man. I paid a hundred dollars. Second
day I got these little scratches again. Might as well kept the
old ones." He thrust the glasses at the first optician.

"They're not scratched," said the first optician. "Just dirty. Your hands are dirty."

The customer flared his nostrils, twitched his cheek, raised his eyebrows. "That's *weak*, Bucket. I come in here show you a pair of glasses get all rubbed and scratched, I'm looking for some *help*. You tell me I need some new glasses. Now the new ones got the *same* problem, you tell me I got dirty *hands*. These the glasses you sold me, my man."

The second optician let air slip very slowly through his tightened lips. "Your old pair was scratched. You had them, what, ten years? They were falling off your face. The hinges were shot, the nosepiece was gone. The lens touched your cheek." He paused to let this litany sink in. "The glasses I sold you are fine. The fit is fine. You just have to break some habits."

"Habits!"

"He's a clown," said the first optician, leaning back against the counter, sticking out his belly. "We should've thrown him out yesterday."

"Instead you took my *money*," hissed the customer. "Good enough for you yesterday. You couldn't see *black* for all the green yesterday. Now I look black to you. Now I'm a clown."

"You think we need your hundred dollars?" The first optician managed a laugh.

"That's not necessary," said the second, to the customer. He ignored his partner. "We'll take care of you. Sit down, let me look at the fit."

"Shit. Your man needs to shut up."

"Okay, please." The second optician pulled up a chair from beside the counter. The padding was pink to match the carpet.

"Sit down."

The partners fell easily into a good optician/bad optician routine. It was pure instinct. Perhaps the customer sensed his options dwindling, perhaps not. Probably he did. The air went out of him a little as he took the chair.

And the glasses, the proof, were in enemy hands. The second optician was rinsing them again.

"Shit, Bucket," said the customer, petulance in his voice now. "What you know about my *habits*?"

"Okay," said the second optician, ignoring the remark. His voice was soothing. "I just want to see you put them on. Just naturally, like you would. Don't push them into your face. They won't fall off. Just drop them over your ears. Then I'll check the fit."

He offered the glasses, then pulled them back as the customer reached for them. "Take off your hat," he said admonishingly.

The customer took off his hat. His hair was grooved where the lip of the hat had rested. The first optician, watching from his place at the counter, reflexively reached up and fluffed his own hair.

"Here you go. Nice and easy." The second optician handed over the glasses.

The customer stuffed the hat in his ass pocket, then raised the glasses with both hands, holding them by the earpieces awkwardly. His hands trembled.

"That's it," said the second optician. "Let's have a look at the fit."

The customer dropped his hands to his lap. The second optician brought his face close to the customer's. For a moment they were still, breathing together tightly, eyes flickering. The intimacy calmed the customer. He was in some sense now getting his due, his money's worth. He could feel the second optician's breath graze his cheek.

Then the second optician saw the marks.

"Wait a minute," said the second optician, straightening his body. "They're still smudged."

"I told you!" said the customer.

"He touched them again," said the first optician, back at the counter. "I told you, he puts his thumb on the lens."

"You touched them again," said the second optician.

"You watched me! You saw! I didn't touch them!"

The second optician shook his head, crestfallen. "I don't understand how it happened."

"Simple, he touched them," said the first.

"Liar!" shouted the customer. "You watched me."

"Listen," said the second optician, rallying, a little frenzied. "This doesn't make sense. What do you think? They smudged themselves? You touched them!"

"I want my money back, Bucket."

"Look, I can give you your money back, it's not going to do any good. You're screwing up your glasses yourself. It's going to be the same wherever you go."

"It's the fit."

"What are you saying, fit?" interrupted the first optician.

"You think they're touching your cheek?"

"That's right. My cheek."

"Show me where," said the first, leaning in.

"For chrissake, don't make him put his hands up there," said the second. The opticians had traded places now, the fierce, the patient. Only the customer was unperturbed, true to himself. He moved his hand with slow drama, like a magician, to point at his face. Shifting and sighing, the opticians closed around him to see.

The rain outside slowed, died. Cars whirred through the water in the street.

"It's my *cheek*," reminded the customer.

"Maybe your last ones touched you there," said the second optician. "Your nosepiece was all worn down. These don't touch."

"I feel it."

"No, you don't. You're used to touching yourself there, putting your fingers in there," said the second. "That's what I meant by habits."

"You don't know," said the customer quietly, with a Buddhist calm. "Now you got to give me my money back."

"We'll see about that," said the second optician grimly. He plucked the glasses from the customer's face.

"This is getting silly," said the first optician to the second. "Give him his money. Get him out of here."

"I'll make him sit here all night if I have to," said the second. "He's putting his fingers on them."

"I got all the time in the world," said the customer happily.

"Sit still," said the second optician. He again dried the glasses with the chamois, and replaced them on the customer's face. "Keep your hands down."

The customer sat, his hands on his knees, the chord of tension in his body stilled at some cost. The second optician leaned in close to the customer's face to inspect the juncture of nosepiece and nose.

"How long are we going to keep him here?" said the first optician pleadingly.

"I told you, as long as it takes."

"You're kidding me."

"Help me watch him. Watch his hands."

The customer smiled, delighted now. He could play this game and win. They'd see the scratches reappear. He focused on his hands. They were all focused on his hands. He kept his hands on his knees.

"We gotta get him out of the way at least," said the first optician.

"Behind the counter," said the second. In his determination he had an answer for everything.

"Here you go, Bucket," said the customer.

"Keep your hands down!" said the second optician. "Let me move the chair. Joe, watch his hands."

The customer was installed behind the counter, hands on his knees, chin up, waiting. The bill of his cap jutted from his back pocket.

The opticians leaned against the wall and the counter,

inspecting the customer as though he were a horse on which they'd bet, and they gamblers looking for some giveaway imperfections, some tremble in its flank.

"He's gonna touch them," said the first optician.

"He *wants* to," said the second. "But he knows we're watching."

"You'll see," said the customer.

"Look at his hands," said the first. "He can't take it, he's gotta go up there. It's like a tic, a whatchamacallit. He's got like Tourette's syndrome or something."

"Fuck you, motherfucker," said the customer genially.

"We've got forever," said the second optician, his tone smooth, his calm restored. "We'll wait it out."

The door chimed. They all turned. The new customer was young, in his late twenties. A boy to these men, a boy in a sweater. He turned to the glass shelves on the wall.

"Can I help you find something?" said the second optician, stepping up. Then he turned and hissed: "Watch his hands!"

"Just browsing," said the new customer, and immediately wondered: Was browsing the right word for glasses? And: Who was that black man in the chair?

"You have glasses before?" asked the second optician.

"Yes, uh, I don't always wear them."

"You want to see anything, let me know."

"Okay."

The new customer moved along the wall of frames, searching for the expensive ones, the Japanese titanium-alloy designs.

Almost involuntarily, he glanced back, and the black man in the chair bugged his eyes at him. A plea for help?

The two opticians in their white coats, gold glasses, and puffy hair reminded him of Nazis. Nazi doctors. Or perhaps Mafia. Yes, definitely Mafia. He'd heard about this neighborhood. He knew of the dark old economic engines still humming away under the bright yuppie surface.

But should he get involved?

He slid closer along the back wall and had another look. The black man sat with his hands on his knees, obviously containing himself. His keepers' eyes shifted from their prisoner to the new customer, watching. What was it they'd said—*Watch his hands*?

"Are you okay?" the new customer blurted.

"Fuck you think, jackass? Fuck you staring at? You see something wrong with me?"

The black man gesticulated, waving the new customer away, and the second optician said: "The hands, the hands."

"What's wrong with his hands?" said the new customer, even as he backed away.

"Mind your own business," said the first optician.

"Damn. He thinks I'm a shoplifter, Bucket. Fucking racist motherfucker."

"I'm sorry."

"Tell him, Bucket. I'm a paying customer."

"It's okay," said the new customer, moving to the door, and out, into the dying afternoon. The sun had arrived just to depart, to throw a few long shadows around as though it had worked the whole day.

The three of them watched the new customer disappear from view of the shop window.

"Now you're scaring off our customers," said the second optician fondly.

"Screw him," said the first optician, waving dismissively at the door. "He was a looker. Just browsing, you heard him."

"Racist jackass got to go jumping to conclusions," said the customer, fingers bouncing on his knees.

"Let me see your hands," said the first optician.

"You got eyes!"

"No, I mean turn them over. Let me take a look."

The customer furrowed his brow. The first optician took the customer's left hand in his own and gently turned it over.

"You're got very rough hands," said the first optician. "Look at your fingertips. Very rough."

The second optician bent in to look, and so did the customer, their heads all drawing together.

"See that?" said the first optician. "Think he could of scratched up his lenses with his fingers like that?"

"Hmmm," said the second optician. "Plastic lenses, sure. Like his old ones. Not glass. Only smudge glass."

"*If* I touched it," said the customer.

"Yeah, right, *if,*" said the first optician, still holding the customer's hand. "We're suspending judgment."

"That's what makes you a good man," said the customer. "You want to do the right thing."

"Yes we do," said the first optician. "That's why we're sitting here. Long as it takes."

"Don't want to go jumping to no conclusions."

"Never."

"Damn straight."

The first optician went to the counter and took out a pack of cigarettes. The second optician sighed.

"You got a good man here, Bucket," said the customer, pointing. "I spoke too soon."

"Watch your hands," said the second optician.

"You'll watch 'em for me, Bucket. I know you will."

The sun was down. Shops outside rolled down their gates. Restaurant deliverymen on green bicycles began to fill the street. Men dragged home milk and flowers and shuttered umbrellas.

The first optician lit another cigarette and put it in the customer's mouth for him, so the customer could keep his hands on his knees.

The second optician moved into the back of the shop, to call his wife, to say he'd be late.

The Dystopianist, Thinking of His Rival, Is Interrupted by a Knock on the Door

THE DYSTOPIANIST DESTROYED THE WORLD again that morning, before making any phone calls or checking his mail, before even breakfast. He destroyed it by cabbages. The Dystopianist's scribbling fingers pushed notes onto the page: a protagonist, someone, *a tousle-haired, well-intentioned geneticist*, had designed a new kind of cabbage for use as a safety device—*the "air bag cabbage."* The air bag cabbage mimicked those decorative cabbages planted by the sides of roads to spell names of towns, or arranged by color—red, white, and that eerie, iridescent cabbage indigo—to create American flags. It looked like any other cabbage. But underground was a network of gas-bag roots, *vast inflatable roots*, filled with pressurized air. So, *at the slightest tap*, no, more than a tap, or vandals would set them off for fun, right, *given a serious blow such as only a car traveling at thirty miles or more per hour could deliver*, the heads of the air bag cabbages would instantly inflate, drawing air from the root system, to cushion the impact of the crash, saving lives, *preventing costly property loss.* Only—

The Dystopianist pushed away from his desk, and squinted through the blinds at the sun-splashed street below. School buses lined his block every morning, like vast tipped orange-juice cartons spilling out the human vitamin of youthful lunacy, that chaos of jeering voices and dancing tangled shadows in the long morning light. The Dystopianist was hungry for breakfast. He didn't know yet how the misguided safety cabbages fucked up the world. He couldn't say what *grievous chain of circumstances* led from the *innocuous genetic novelty* to another *crushing totalitarian regime.* He didn't know what light the cabbages shed on the *death urge in human societies.* He'd work it out, though. That was his job. First Monday of each month the Dystopianist came up with his idea, the *green poison fog* or *dehumanizing fractal download* or *alienating architectural fad* which would open the way to another ruined or oppressed reality. Tuesday he began making his extrapolations, and he had the rest of the month to get it right. Today was Monday, so the cabbages were enough.

The Dystopianist moved into the kitchen, poured a second cup of coffee, and pushed slices of bread into the toaster. The *Times* Metro section headline spoke of the capture of a celebrated villain, an addict and killer who'd crushed a pedestrian's skull with a cobblestone. The Dystopianist read his paper while scraping his toast with shreds of ginger marmalade, knife rushing a little surf of butter ahead of the crystalline goo. He read intently to the end of the account, taking pleasure in the story.

The Dystopianist hated bullies. He tried to picture himself standing behind darkened glass, fingering perps in a line-up, couldn't. He tried to picture himself standing in the glare, head flinched in arrogant dejection, waiting to be fingered, but this was even more impossible. He stared at the photo of the apprehended man and unexpectedly the Dystopianist found himself thinking vengefully, hatefully, of his rival.

Once the Dystopianist had had the entire dystopian field to himself. There was just him and the Utopianists. The Dystopianist loved reading the Utopianists' stories, their dim, hopeful scenarios, which were published in magazines like *Expectant* and *Encouraging*. The Dystopianist routinely purchased them newly minted from the newsstands and perverted them the very next day in his own work, plundering the Utopianists' motifs for dark inspiration. Even the garishly sunny illustrated covers of the magazines were fuel. The Dystopianist stripped them from the magazines' spines and pinned them up over his desk, then raised his pen like Death's sickle and plunged those dreamily ineffectual worlds into ruin.

The Utopianists were older men who'd come into the field from the sciences or from academia: Professor this or that, like Dutch burghers from a cigar box. The Dystopianist had appeared in print like a rat among them, a burrowing animal laying turds on their never-to-be-realized blueprints. He liked his role. Every once in a blue moon the Dystopianist agreed to appear in public alongside the Utopianists, on a panel at a university or a conference. They loved to gather, *the fools*, in fluorescent-lit halls behind tables decorated with sweating pitchers of ice water. They were always eager to praise him in public by calling him one of their own. The Dystopianist ignored them, refusing even the water from their pitchers. He played directly to the audience members who'd come to see him, who shared his low opinion of the Utopianists. The Dystopianist could always spot his readers by their black trench coats, their acne, their greasily teased hair, their earphones, resting around their collars, trailing to Walkmans secreted in coat pockets.

The Dystopianist's rival was a Utopianist, but he wasn't like the others.

The Dystopianist had known his rival, the man he privately called *the Dire One*, since they were children like those streaming into the schoolyard below. *Eeny meeny miney moe!* they'd chanted together, each trembling in fear of being permanently "*It*," of never casting off their permanent case of *cooties*. They weren't quite friends, but the Dystopianist and the Dire One had been bullied together by the older boys, quarantined in their shared nerdishness, forced to pool their resentments. In glum resignation they'd swapped Wacky Packages stickers and algebra homework answers, offered sticks of Juicy Fruit and squares of Now-N-Later, forging a loser's deal of consolation.

Then they were separated after junior high school, and the Dystopianist forgot his uneasy schoolmate.

It was nearly a year now since the Dire Utopianist had first arrived in print. The Dystopianist had trundled home with the latest issue of *Heartening*, expecting the usual laughs, and been blindsided instead by the Dire Utopianist's first story. The Dystopianist didn't recognize his rival by name, but he knew him for a rival instantly.

The Dire Utopianist's trick was to write in a style which was *nominally* utopian. His fantasies were nearly as credible as everyday experience, but bathed in a radiance of glory. They glowed with wishfulness. The other Utopianists' stories were crude candy floss by comparison. The Dire Utopianist's stories weren't blunt or ideological. He'd invented an *aesthetics* of utopia.

Fair enough. If he'd stopped at this burnished, closely observed dream of human life, the Dire Utopianist would be no threat. Sure, heck, let there be one genius among the Utopianists, all the better. It raised the bar. The Dystopianist took the Dire One's mimetic brilliance as a spur of inspiration: Look closer! Make it real!

But the Dire Utopianist didn't play fair. He didn't stop at utopianism, no. He poached on the Dystopianist's turf, he encroached. By limning a world so subtly transformed, so barely *nudged* into the ideal, the Dire One's fictions cast a shadow back onto the everyday. They induced a despair of inadequacy in the real. Turning the last page of one of the Dire Utopianist's stories, the reader felt a mortal pang at slipping back into his own daily life, which had been proved morbid, crushed, unfair.

This was the Dire One's pitiless art: *his utopias wrote reality itself into the most persuasive dystopia imaginable.* At the Dystopianist's weak moments he knew his stories were by comparison contrived and crotchety, their darkness forced.

It was six weeks ago that *Vivifying* had published the Dire One's photograph, and the Dystopianist had recognized his childhood acquaintance.

The Dire Utopianist never appeared in public. There was no clamor for him to appear. In fact, he wasn't even particularly esteemed among the Utopianists, an irony which rankled the Dystopianist. It was as though the Dire One didn't mind seeing his work buried in the insipid utopian magazines. He didn't seem to crave recognition of any kind, let alone the hard-won oppositional stance the Dystopianist treasured. It was almost as though the Dire One's stories, posted in public, were really private messages of reproach from one man to the other. Sometimes the Dystopianist wondered if he were in fact the *only* reader the Dire Utopianist had, and the only one he wanted.

The cabbages were hopeless, the Dystopianist saw now.

Gazing out the window over his coffee's last plume of steam at the humming, pencil-colored school buses, he suddenly understood the gross implausibility: a rapidly inflating cabbage could never have the *stopping power* to *alter the fatal trajectory* of a *careening steel egg carton full of young lives*. A cabbage might halt a Hyundai, maybe a Volvo. Never a school bus. Anyway, the cabbages as an image had no implications, no *reach*. They said nothing about mankind. They were, finally, completely stupid and lame. He gulped the last of his coffee, angrily.

He had to go deeper, find something resonant, something to crawl beneath the skin of reality and render it monstrous from within. He paced to the sink, began rinsing his coffee mug. A tiny pod of silt had settled at the bottom and now, under a jet of cold tap water, the grains rose and spread and danced, a model of chaos. The Dystopianist retraced his seed of inspiration: *well-intentioned, bumbling geneticist*, good. Good enough. The geneticist needed to stumble onto something better, though.

One day, when the Dystopianist and the Dire Utopianist had been in the sixth grade at Intermediate School 293, cowering together in a corner of the schoolyard to duck sports and fights and girls in one deft multipurpose cower, they had arrived at a safe island of mutual interest: comic books, Marvel brand, which anyone who read them understood weren't comic at all but deadly, breathtakingly serious. Marvel constructed worlds of splendid complexity, full of chilling, ancient villains and tormented heroes, in richly unfinished story lines. There in the schoolyard, wedged for cover behind the girls' lunch-hour game of hopscotch, the Dystopianist declared his favorite character: Doctor Doom, antagonist of the Fantastic Four. Doctor Doom wore a forest green cloak and hood over a metallic slitted mask and armor. He was a dark king who from his gnarled castle ruled a city of hapless serfs. An imperial, self-righteous monster. The Dire Utopianist murmured his consent. Indeed, Doctor Doom was awesome, an honorable choice. The Dystopianist waited for the Dire Utopianist to declare his favorite.

"Black Bolt," said the Dire Utopianist.

The Dystopianist was confused. Black Bolt wasn't a villain or a hero. Black Bolt was part of an outcast band of mutant characters known as the Inhumans, the noblest among them. He was their leader, but he never spoke. His only *demonstrated* power was flight, but the whole point of Black Bolt was the power he restrained himself from using: speech. The sound of his voice was cataclysmic, an unusable weapon, like an atomic bomb. If Black Bolt ever uttered a syllable the world would crack in two. Black Bolt was leader in absentia much of the time—he had a tendency to exile himself from the scene, to wander distant mountaintops contemplating . . . What? His curse? The things he would say if he could safely speak?

It was an unsettling choice there, amidst the feral shrieks of the schoolyard. The Dystopianist changed the subject, and never raised the question of Marvel Comics with the Dire Utopianist again. Alone behind the locked door of his bedroom the Dystopianist studied Black Bolt's behavior, seeking hints of the character's appeal to his schoolmate. Perhaps the answer lay in a story line elsewhere in the Marvel universe, one where Black Bolt shucked off his pensiveness to function as an unrestrained hero or villain. If so, the Dystopianist never found the comic book in question.

Suicide, the Dystopianist concluded now. The geneticist should be studying suicide, seeking to isolate it as a factor in the human genome. "The Sylvia Plath Code," that might be the title of the story. The geneticist could be trying to *reproduce it in a nonhuman species*. Right, good. To breed for suicide in animals, to produce a creature with the impulse to take its own life. That had the relevance the Dystopianist was looking for. What animals? Something poignant and pathetic, something pure. Sheep. *The Sylvia Plath Sheep*, that was it.

A variant of sheep had been bred for the study of sui-cide. The Sylvia Plath Sheep had to be kept on close watch, like a prisoner stripped of sharp implements, shoelaces, and belt. And the Plath Sheep escapes, right, of course, *a Frankenstein creature always escapes*, but the twist is that the Plath Sheep is dangerous only to itself. *So what?* What harm if a single sheep quietly, discreetly offs itself? *But the Plath Sheep*, scribbling fingers racing now, the Dystopianist was on fire, *the Plath Sheep turns out to have the gift of communicating its despair*. Like the monkeys on that island, who learned from one another to wash clams, or break them open with coconuts, whatever it was the monkeys had learned, look into it later, *the Plath Sheep evoked suicide in other creatures*, all up and down the food chain. Not humans, but anything else that crossed its path. Cats, dogs, cows, beetles, clams. Each creature would spread suicide to another, to five or six others, before *searching out a promontory from which to plunge to its death*. The human species would be powerless to reverse the craze, the epidemic of suicide among the nonhuman species of the planet.

Okay! Right! Let goddamn Black Bolt open his mouth and sing an aria—he couldn't halt the Plath Sheep in its *deadly spiral of despair!*

The Dystopianist suddenly had a vision of the Plath Sheep wandering its way into the background of one of the Dire One's tales. It would go unremarked at first, a bucolic detail. Unwrapping its bleak gift of *global animal suicide* only after it had been taken entirely for granted, just as the Dire One's own little nuggets of despair were smuggled innocuously into his utopias. The Plath Sheep was a bullet of pure dystopian intention. The Dystopianist wanted to fire it in the Dire Utopianist's direction. Maybe he'd send this story to *Encouraging*.

Even better, he'd like it if he could send the Plath Sheep itself to the door of the Dire One's writing room. *Here's your tragic mute Black Bolt, you bastard!* Touch its somber muzzle, dry its moist obsidian eyes, runny with sleep goo. Try to talk it down from the parapet, if you have the courage of your ostensibly rosy convictions. Explain to the Sylvia Plath Sheep why life is worth living. Or, failing that, let the sheep convince you to follow it up to the brink, and go. You and the sheep, pal, take a fall.

There was a knock on the door.

The Dystopianist went to the door and opened it. Standing in the corridor was a sheep. The Dystopianist checked his watch—nine forty-five. He wasn't sure why it mattered to him what time it was, but it did. He found it reassuring. The day still stretched before him; he'd have plenty of time to resume work after this interruption. He still heard the children's voices leaking in through the front window from the street below. The children arriving now were late for school. There were always hundreds who were late. He wondered if the sheep had waited with the children for the crossing guard to wave it on. He wondered if the sheep had crossed at the green, or recklessly dared the traffic to kill it.

He'd persuaded himself that the sheep was voiceless. So it was a shock when it spoke. "May I come in?" said the sheep.

"Yeah, sure," said the Dystopianist, fumbling his words. Should he offer the sheep the couch, or a drink of something? The sheep stepped into the apartment, just far enough to allow the door to be closed behind it, then stood quietly working its nifty little jaw back and forth, and blinking. Its eyes were not watery at all.

"So," said the sheep, nodding its head at the Dystopianist's desk, the mass of yellow legal pads, the sharpened pencils bunched in their holder, the typewriter. "This is where the magic happens." The sheep's tone was wearily sarcastic.

"It isn't usually *magic*," said the Dystopianist, then immediately regretted the remark.

"Oh, I wouldn't say that," said the sheep, apparently unruffled. "You've got a few things to answer for."

"Is that what this is?" said the Dystopianist. "Some kind of reckoning?"

"Reckoning?" The sheep blinked as though confused. "Who said anything about a reckoning?"

"Never mind," said the Dystopianist. He didn't want to put words into the sheep's mouth. Not now. He'd let it represent itself, and try to be patient.

But the sheep didn't speak, only moved in tiny, faltering steps on the carpet, advancing very slightly into the room. The Dystopianist wondered if the sheep might be scouting for sharp corners on the furniture, for chances to do itself harm by butting with great force against his fixtures.

"Are you—very depressed?" asked the Dystopianist.

The sheep considered the question for a moment. "I've had better days, let's put it that way."

Finishing the thought, it stared up at him, eyes still dry. The Dystopianist met its gaze, then broke away. A terrible thought occurred to him: the sheep might be expecting *him* to relieve it of its life.

The silence was ponderous. The Dystopianist considered another possibility. Might his rival have come to him in disguised form?

He cleared his throat before speaking. "You're not, ah, the Dire One, by any chance?" The Dystopianist was going to be awfully embarrassed if the sheep didn't know what he was talking about.

The sheep made a solemn, wheezing sound, like

Hurrrrhh. Then it said, "I'm *dire* all right. But I'm hardly the only one."

"Who?" blurted the Dystopianist.

"Take a look in the mirror, friend."

"What's your point?" The Dystopianist was sore now. If the sheep thought he was going to be manipulated into suicide it had *another think coming.*

"Just this: How many sheep have to die to assuage your childish resentments?" Now the sheep assumed an odd false tone, bluff like that of a commercial pitchman: *"They laughed when I sat down at the Dystopiano! But when I began to play—"*

"Very funny."

"We try, we try. Look, could you at least offer me a dish of water or something? I had to take the stairs—couldn't reach the button for the elevator."

Silenced, the Dystopianist hurried into the kitchen and filled a shallow bowl with water from the tap. Then, thinking twice, he poured it back into the sink and replaced it with mineral water from the bottle in the door of his refrigerator. When he set it out the sheep lapped gratefully, steadily, seeming to the Dystopianist an animal at last.

"Okay." It licked its lips. "That's it, Doctor Doom. I'm out of here. Sorry for the intrusion, next time I'll call. I just wanted, you know—a look at you."

The Dystopianist couldn't keep from saying, "You don't want to die?"

"Not today," was the sheep's simple reply. The Dystopianist stepped carefully around the sheep to open the

door, and the sheep trotted out. The Dystopianist trailed
it into the corridor and summoned the elevator. When the
cab arrived and the door opened the Dystopianist leaned
in and punched the button for the lobby.

"Thanks," said the sheep. "It's the little things that
count."

The Dystopianist tried to think of a proper farewell,
but couldn't before the elevator door shut. The sheep was
facing the rear of the elevator cab, another instance of its
poor grasp of etiquette.

Still, the sheep's visit wasn't the worst the Dystopianist
could imagine. It could have attacked him, or tried to gore
itself on his kitchen knives. The Dystopianist was still
proud of the Plath Sheep, and rather glad to have met it,
even if the Plath Sheep wasn't proud of him. Besides, the
entire episode had only cost the Dystopianist an hour or
so of his time. He was back at work, eagerly scribbling out
implications, extrapolations, another illustrious downfall,
well before the yelping children reoccupied the schoolyard
at lunchtime.

Super Goat Man

WHEN SUPER GOAT MAN MOVED INTO THE commune on our street I was ten years old. Though I liked superheroes, I wasn't familiar with Super Goat Man. His presence didn't mean anything, particularly, to myself or to the other kids in the neighborhood. For us, as we ran and screamed and played secret games on the sidewalk, Super Goat Man was only another of the men who sat on stoops in sleeveless undershirts on hot summer days, watching the slow progress of life on the block. The two little fleshy horns on his forehead didn't make him especially interesting. We weren't struck by his fall from grace, out of the world of comic-book heroes, among which he had been at best a minor star, to land here in Cobble Hill, Brooklyn, in a single room in what was basically a dorm for college dropouts, a hippie group shelter, any more than we were by the tufts of extra hair at his throat and behind his ears. We had eyes only for Spider-Man or Batman in those days, superheroes in two dimensions, with lunch boxes and television shows and theme songs. Super Goat Man had none of those.

It was our dads who cared. They were unmistakably drawn to the strange figure who'd moved to the block, as though for them he represented some lost possibility in their own lives. My father in particular seemed fascinated with Super Goat Man, though he covered this interest by acting as though it were on my behalf. One day toward the end of that summer he and I walked to Montague Street, to visit the comics shop there. This was a tiny storefront filled with long white boxes, crates full of carefully archived comics, protected by plastic bags and cardboard backing. The boxes contained ancient runs of back issues of titles I'd heard of, as well as thousands of other comics featuring characters I'd never encountered. The shop was presided over by a nervous young pedant with long hair and a beard, a collector-type himself, an old man in spirit who distrusted children in his store, as he ought to have. He assisted my father in finding what he sought, deep in the alphabetical archive—a five-issue run of *The Remarkable Super Goat Man*, from Electric Comics. These were the only comics in which Super Goat Man had appeared. There were just five issues because after five the title had

been forever canceled. My father seemed satisfied with what he'd found. We paid for the five issues and left.

I didn't know how to explain to my father that Electric wasn't one of the major comics publishers. The stories the comics contained, when we inspected them together, were both ludicrous and boring. Super Goat Man's five issues showed him rescuing old ladies from swerving trucks and kittens from lightning-struck trees, and battling dull villains like Vest Man and False Dave. The drawings were amateurish, cut-rate, antiquated. I couldn't have articulated these judgments then, of course. I only knew I disliked the comics, found them embarrassing, for myself, for Super Goat Man, and for my dad. They languished in my room, unread, and were eventually cleaned up—I mean, thrown out—by my mom.

For the next few years Super Goat Man was less than a minor curiosity to me. I didn't waste thought on him. The younger men and women who lived in the commune took him for granted, as anyone should, so far as I knew. We kids would see him in their company, moving furniture u the stoop and into the house, discarded dressers ar couches and lamps they'd found on the street, or tapi posters on lampposts announcing demonstrations agai nuclear power or in favor of day-care centers, or weed in the commune's pathetic front yard, which was inten as a vegetable garden but was choked not only with u vited growth but with discarded ice-cream wrappers soda bottles—we kids used the commune's yard dumping ground. It didn't occur to me that Super

Man was much older, really, than the commune's other oc-
cupants, that in fact they might be closer to my age than
to his. However childish their behavior, the hippies all
seemed as dull and remote as grown-ups to me.

It was the summer when I was thirteen that my parents
allowed me to accompany them to one of the commune's
potluck dinners. The noise and vibrancy of that house's
sporadic celebrations were impossible to ignore on our
street, and I knew my parents had attended a few earlier
parties—warily, I imagined. The inhabitants of the commune were always trying to sweep their neighbors into dubious causes, and it might be a mistake to be seduced by
frivolity into some sticky association. But my parents liked
fun too. And had too little of it. Their best running jokes
concerned the dullness of their friends' dinner parties.
This midsummer evening they brought me along to see inside the life of the scandalous, anomalous house.

The house was already full, many bearded and jeweled
and scruffy, reeking of patchouli and musk, others, like
my parents, dressed in their hippest collarless shirts and
paisley blouses, wearing their fattest beads and bracelets.
The offerings, nearly all casseroles brimming with exotic
gray proteins, beans and tofu and eggplant and more I
couldn't name, were lined on a long side table, mostly ignored. This was a version of cocktail hour, with beer
drunk from the bottle and well-rolled marijuana cigarettes. I didn't see whether my parents indulged in the lat-
ter. My mother accepted a glass of orange juice, surely
spiked. I meant not to pay them any attention, so I moved

for the stairs. There were partiers leaning on the banister at the first landing, and evidence of music playing in upstairs rooms, so I didn't doubt the whole house was open to wandering.

There was no music coming from the garden-facing room on the second floor, but the door was open and three figures were visible inside, seated on cushions on a mattress on the floor. A young couple, and Super Goat Man. From his bare hairy feet on the mattress, I guessed it was his room I'd entered. The walls were sparse apart from a low bookcase, on which I spotted, laid crosswise in the row of upright spines, Norman Mailer's *Armies of the Night*, Sergei Eisenstein's *Film Form / The Film Sense*, and Thomas Pynchon's *V*. The three titles stuck in my head; I would later attempt to read each of the three at college, succeeding only with the Mailer. Beside the bookcase was a desk heaped with papers, and behind it a few black-and-white postcards had been thumbtacked to the wall. These looked less like a considered decoration than as if they'd been pinned up impulsively by a sitter at the desk. One of the postcard images I recognized as Charlie Parker, clutching a saxophone with his meaty hands. The jazzman was an idol of my father's, perhaps a symbol of his vanished youth.

The young man on the mattress was holding a book: *Memories, Dreams, Reflections*, by Carl Jung. Super Goat Man had evidently just pressed it on him, and had likely been extolling its virtues when I walked into the room.

"Hello," said the young woman, her voice warm. I must

have been staring, from my place in the middle of the room.

"You're Everett, aren't you?" said Super Goat Man, before I could speak.

"How'd you know my name?"

"You live on the block," said Super Goat Man. "I've seen you running around."

"I think we'll head down, Super Goat Man," said the young man abruptly, tucking the book under his arm as he got up from the mattress. "Get something to eat before it's too late."

"I want to hit the dance floor," said the young woman.

"See you down there," said Super Goat Man. With that the young couple were gone.

"You checking out the house?" said Super Goat Man to me once we were alone. "Casing the joint?"

"I'm looking for my friend," I lied.

"I think some kids are hanging out in the backyard."

"No, she went upstairs." I wanted him to think I had a girlfriend.

"Okay, cool," said Super Goat Man. He smiled. I suppose he was waiting for me to leave, but he didn't give any sign that I was bothering him by staying.

"Why do you live here?" I asked.

"These are my friends," he said. "They helped me out when I lost my job."

"You're not a superhero anymore, are you?"

Super Goat Man shrugged. "Some people felt I was

being too outspoken about the war. Anyway, I wanted to accomplish things on a more local level."

"Why don't you have a secret identity?"

"I wasn't that kind of superhero."

"But what was your name, before?"

"Ralph Gersten."

"What did Ralph Gersten do?"

"He was a college teacher, for a couple of years."

"So why aren't you Ralph Gersten now?"

"Sometime around when they shot Kennedy I just realized Ralph Gersten wasn't who I was. He was a part of an old life I was holding on to. So I became Super Goat Man. I've come to understand that this is who I am, for better or worse."

This was a bit much for me to assimilate, so I changed the subject. "Do you smoke pot?"

"Sometimes."

"Were Mr. and Mrs. Gersten sad when you gave up your secret identity?"

"Who?"

"Your parents."

Super Goat Man smiled. "They weren't my real parents. I was adopted."

Suddenly I was done. "I'm going downstairs, Super Goat Man."

"Okay, Everett," he said. "See you down there, probably."

I made my way downstairs, and lurked in the commune's muddy and ill-lit backyard, milling with the other teenagers and children stranded there by the throngs of frolickers—for the party was now overflowing its bounds, and we were free to steal beers from the counter and carry on our own tentative party, our own fumbling flirtations. I had no girlfriend, but I did play spin the bottle that night, crouched on the ground beneath a fig tree.

Then, near midnight, I went back inside. The living room was jammed with bodies—dancers on a parquet floor that had been revealed when the vast braided rug had been curled up against the base of the mantel. Colored Christmas lights were bunched in the corner, and some of them blinked to create a gently eerie strobe. I smelled sweat and smoke. Feeling perverse and thrilled by the kisses I'd exchanged in the mud beneath the tree, I meandered into the web of celebrants.

Super Goat Man was there. He was dancing with my mother. She was as I'd never seen her, braceleted wrists crossed above her head, swaying to the reggae—I think it was the sound track to *The Harder They Come*. Super Goat Man was more dressed-up than he'd been in his room upstairs. He wore a felt brocade vest and striped pants. He danced in tiny little steps, almost as though losing and regaining his balance, his arms loose at his sides, fingers snapping. Mostly he moved his head to the beat, shaking it back and forth as if saying *no-no-no, no-no-no*. He shook his head at my mother's dancing, as if he couldn't approve of the way she was moving, but couldn't quit paying attention either.

My father? He was seated on the rolled-up rug, his back against the mantel, elbows on his knees, dangling with forefinger and thumb a nearly empty paper cup of red wine. Like me, he was watching my mom and Super Goat Man. It didn't look as if it bothered him at all.

. . .

MY JUNIOR year at Corcoran College, in Corcoran, New Hampshire, Super Goat Man was brought in to fill the Walt Whitman Chair in the Humanities. This was 1981, the dawn of Reagan. The chair was required to offer one course; Super Goat Man's was listed in the catalogue as Dissidence and Desire: Marginal Heroics in American Life 1955–1975. The reading included Frantz Fanon, Roland Barthes, and Timothy Leary. It was typical of Corcoran that it would choose that particular moment to recuperate a figure associated with sixties protest, to enshrine what had once been at the vigorous center of the culture in the harmless pantheon of academia. It was Super Goat Man's first teaching job since the fifties. The commune on our street had shut down at some point in my high-school years, and I don't know where Super Goat Man had been in the intervening time. I certainly hadn't thought about him since departing for college.

He'd gained a little weight, but was otherwise unchanged. I first spotted him moving across the Commons lawn on a September afternoon, one with the scent of fallen and fermenting crab apples on the breeze. It was one of those rare, sweet days on either side of the long New Hampshire winter, when a school year was either falsely fresh before its plunge into bleak December, or exhausted and ready to give way to summer. Super Goat Man wore a forest green corduroy suit and a wide salmon tie, but his feet were still bare. A couple of Corcoran girls trailed alongside him. He had a book open as he walked—perhaps he was reading them a poem.

The college had assigned Super Goat Man one of the dormitory apartments—a suite of rooms built into Sweeney House, one of the student residences. That is to say, he lived on the edge of the vast commons lawn, and we students felt his watchful presence much as I had in Cobble Hill, on our street. I didn't take Super Goat Man's class, which was mostly full of freshmen, and of those renegade history and rhetoric majors who'd been seduced by French strains of philosophy and literary theory. I fancied myself a classics scholar then—though I'd soon divert into a major in history—and wasn't curious about contemporary political theory, even if I'd believed Super Goat Man to be a superior teacher, which I didn't. I wasn't certain he had nothing to offer the Corcoran students, but whatever it might be it wasn't summed up by the title of his class.

I did, however, participate in one of the late-night salons in the living room of Sweeney House. Super Goat Man had begun appearing there casually, showing up after a few students had occupied the couches, and had lit a fire or opened a bottle of red wine. Increasingly his presence was relied upon; soon it was a given that he was the center of an unnamed tradition. Though Corcoran College was then in the throes of a wave of glamorous eighties-style binge parties, and cocaine had begun to infiltrate our sanctum in the New Hampshire woods as if we were all denizens of Andy Warhol's Factory, the Sweeney House salons were a throwback to another, earlier temperature of college socializing. Bearded art students who disdained dancing in favor of bull sessions, Woolfian-Plathian girls in long antique dresses, and lonely gay virgins of both genders—these were the types who found their way to Sweeney to sit at Super Goat Man's feet. There were also, from what I observed, a handful of quiet superhero comic-book fans who revered Super Goat Man in that capacity and were covertly basking in his aura, ashamed to ask the sorts of questions I'd peppered him with in his room in the communal house, so long ago.

The evening I sat in, Super Goat Man had dragged his phonograph out from his apartment and set it up in the living room so that he could play Lenny Bruce records for his acolytes. Super Goat Man had five or six of the records. He spoke intermittently, his voice unhurried and reflective, explaining the context of the famous comedian's arrests and courtroom battles before dropping the needle on a given track. After a while conversation drifted to other subjects. Cross talk arose, though whenever Super Goat Man began to speak in his undemonstrative way all chatter fell deferentially silent. Then Super Goat Man went into his apartment and brought out an Ornette Coleman LP.

"You know a bit about jazz, don't you, Everett?" It was the first time he'd addressed me directly. I hadn't known he'd recognized me.

"A thing or two, I guess."

"Everett's father was the one who turned me on to Rahsaan Roland Kirk," Super Goat Man told a teenager I recognized, a bespectacled sophomore who'd impressively talked his way into a classics seminar that was meant for upperclassmen. "I always thought that stuff was too gimmicky, but I'd never really listened."

I tried to imagine when Super Goat Man and my dad had spent so much time together. It was almost impossible to picture, but Super Goat Man didn't have any reason to be lying about it. It was one of the first times I was forced to consider the possibility that my parents had social lives—that they had lives.

"Does your father write about jazz?" the sophomore asked me, wide-eyed. I suppose he'd misunderstood Super Goat Man's remark. There were plenty of famous—or at least interesting—fathers at Corcoran College, but mine wasn't one of them.

"My father works for New York State," I said. "Department of Housing and Urban Development. Well, he just lost his job, in fact."

"He's a good five-card-stud player too," said Super

Goat Man. "Cleaned me out a few times, I don't mind saying."

"Oh yeah, my dad's a real supervillain," I said with the heaviest sarcasm I could muster. I was embarrassed to think of my father sucking up to Super Goat Man, as he surely had during their long evenings together, whoever had taken the bulk of the chips.

Then the squeaky jazz began playing, and Super Goat Man, though seated in one of the dormitory's ratty arm-chairs, closed his eyes and began shaking his head as if transported back to the commune's dance floor, or perhaps to some even earlier time. I studied his face. The tufts around his ears and throat were graying. I puzzled over his actual age. Had Super Goat Man once spent decades frozen in a block of ice, like Captain America? If Ralph Gersten had been a college teacher in the fifties, he was probably older than my dad.

Eight months later the campus was green again. The term was almost finished, all of us nearly freed to summer, when it happened: the incident at the Campanile. A Saturday, late in a balmy night of revels, the Commons lawn full of small groups crossing from dorm to dorm, cruising at the parties which still flared like bonfires in the landscape of the campus. Many of us yet owed papers, others would have to sit in a final class the following Monday, but the mood was one of expulsive release from our labors. It was nearly three in the morning when Rudy Krugerrand and Seth Brummell, two of the wealthiest and most widely

reviled frat boys at Corcoran, scaled the Campanile tower
and began bellowing.

I was among those awake and near enough by to be
drawn by the commotion, into the small crowd at the dark
base of the Campanile tower. When I first gazed up at
Rudy and Seth I was confused by what I saw: Were there
four figures spotlit against the clock beneath the bells?
And where were the campus authorities? It was as though
this night had been officially ceded to some bacchanalian
imperative.

That spring a sculpture student had, as his thesis project, decorated the Commons with oversize office sup-
plies—a stapler in the dimensions of a limousine, a log
painted as a number two pencil, and a pile of facsimile paper clips each the height of a human being, fashioned out
of plastic piping and silver paint. I suppose the work was
derivative of Claes Oldenburg, but the result made an im-
pressive spectacle. It was two of the paper-clip sculptures
that Rudy Krugerrand and Seth Brummell had managed
to attach to their belts like mannequin dance partners and
drag with them out onto the ledge of the Campanile clock,
where they stood now, six stories from the ground. On the
precipice at the clockface, their faces uplit in the flood-
lights, Rudy and Seth were almost like players in the climax of some Gothic silent-film drama, but they didn't
have the poise or imagination to know it. They were only
college pranksters, reelingly drunk, Seth with a three-
quarters empty bottle of Jack Daniels still in his hand, and
at first it was hard to make out what they were shouting.

We on the ground predictably shouted *"Jump!"* back at them, knowing they loved themselves too dearly ever to consider it.

Then Rudy Krugerrand's slurred voice rose out above the din—or perhaps it was only that I picked it out of the din for the first time. "Calling Super Goat Man! Calling Super Goat Man!" He shouted this until his voice broke hoarse. "This looks like a job for Super Goat Man! Come out, come out, wherever you are!"

"What's going on?" I asked a student beside me.

He shrugged. "I guess they're calling out Super Goat Man. They want to see if he can get them down from the ledge."

"What do you mean?"

"They want to see him use his powers."

From the clock tower Seth Brummell screamed now, in a girlish falsetto: "Oh, Super Goat Man, where are you?"

A stirring had begun in the crowd, which had grown by now to a hundred or more. A murmuring. Super Goat Man's name was planted like a seed. Under the guise of concern for Rudy and Seth, but certainly with a shiver of voyeuristic anticipation, some had begun to speak of going to the Sweeney House apartment, to see if Super Goat Man could be located. There was a hint of outrage: Why wasn't he here already? What kind of Super Goat Man was he, anyway?

Now a group of fifteen or twenty broke out and streamed down the hill, toward Sweeney House. Others trailed after them, myself included. I hid in this crowd, feeling like an observer, though I suppose I was as complicit as anyone. Were we only curious, or a part of a mob? It seemed, anyway, that we were under the direction of Rudy and Seth.

"That's right," mocked Rudy. "Only Super Goat Man can save us now!"

Those who'd led the charge hammered on Super Goat Man's apartment door for a good few minutes before getting a result. Bold enough to have woken him, they inched backward at the sight of him on his threshold, dressed only in a flowery silk kimono, blinking groggily at the faces arrayed on the hill. Then someone stepped forward and took his arm, pointed him toward the Campanile. Any conversation was drowned in murmurs, and by the sound of sirens, now belatedly pulling up at the base of the tower. Super Goat Man shook his head sorrowfully, but he began to trek up the hill to the Commons, toward the Campanile. We all fell in around and behind him, emboldened at marching to the beat of a superhero's step, feeling the pulse of the script it now appeared would be played out, ignoring the fact that it had been written by Rudy and Seth and Jack Daniels. Super Goat Man's kimono fluttered slightly, not quite a cape. He tightened the sash, and strode, rubbing at his eyes with balled fists.

This success only seemed to enrage Rudy and Seth, who writhed and scorned from atop their perch. "Baaahh, baaahh, Super Goat Man!" they roared. "What's the matter with your goaty senses? Smoke too much dope tonight? *Fuck* you, Super Goat Man!" Seth lifted his giant paper clip above his head, to shake it like a fake strongman's prop dumbbell.

The campus police began to herd the students from the base of the tower, but our arriving throng pushed the opposite way. In the confusion, the young policemen seemed utterly helpless, and fell back. Straining on tiptoe to see over the heads of the crowd, I followed the progress of the lime green kimono as Super Goat Man was thrust to the fore, not necessarily by his own efforts. Above, Seth was strumming air-guitar chords on his paper clip, then waggling it over our heads like an enormous phallus.

"Bite my crank, Super Goat Man!"

The crowd gasped as Super Goat Man shed his garb— for mobility I suppose—and started shimmying, almost scampering, up the face of the tower. His pelt was glossy in the moonlight, but nobody could have mistaken the wide swath of white above his dusky buttocks for sheen. Super Goat Man was aging. He scurried through the leaf-blobby shade a tree branch cast against the side of the tower, then back into the light. Whether it was the pressure of expectation on a still-sleepy mind, or possibly a genuine calling to heroics, a hope he could do some good here, Super Goat Man had taken the bait. His limbs worked miraculously in ascending the tower, yet one could only dread what would come if he reached the idiot boys at the top, who grew more agitated and furious at every inch he achieved. Rudy had lifted his own paper clip, to match Seth, and now he swung it out over us.

The plummet silenced us. It was over before we could

swallow our words and form a cry to replace them. Six stories is no distance at all, only enough. Rudy's paper clip had overbalanced him. Super Goat Man had braced three limbs, and reached out with a fourth—some number of us saw, others only imagined afterward—but he didn't come away with Rudy. Super Goat Man caught the paper clip in mid-flight with the prehensile toes of his left foot, and the sculpture was jerked free from Rudy as he fell. That's how firm was Super Goat Man's hold on the tower's third story: it was left for later to speculate whether he might have been able to halt a human body's fall. Rudy came to earth, shattering at the feet of the policemen there at the tower's base. Now the nude furry figure could only undertake a sober, methodical descent, paper clip tucked beneath one arm. At the clockface, Seth Brummell was mute, clinging to a post, to wait for the security men who would soon unlock the small door in the tower behind him and angrily yank him to safety.

Rudy Krugerrand survived his fall. His ruined spine cost him the use of his legs, cost him all feeling below some point at his middle. Only a junior, he rather courageously reappeared in a mechanical wheelchair the following September, resumed his studies, resumed drinking too, though his temperament was mellowed, reflective now. He'd be seen at parties dozing in the corner after the dance floor had filled—it took very little beer to knock his dwindled body out. If Rudy had died, or never returned, the incident likely would have been avidly discussed, etched into campus legend. Instead it was covered in a clumsy hush.

The coexistence in the same small community of Rudy and Super Goat Man—who'd been offered a seat in the social sciences, and accepted—comprised a kind of odd, insoluble puzzle: Had the hero failed the crisis? Caused it, by some innate provocation? Or was the bogus crisis unworthy, and the outcome its own reward? Who'd shamed whom?

I contemplated this koan, or didn't, for just another year. My graduate studies took me to the University of California at Irvine, three thousand grateful miles from Corcoran, now Super Goat Man's province. I didn't see him, or think of him again, for more than a decade.

• • •

THE SWEETEST student I ever had was an Italian girl named Angela Verucci. Tall, bronze-skinned, with a quizzical, slightly humorless cast, dressed no matter the weather in neat pantsuits or skirts with stockings, in heavy tortoise-shell glasses frames and with her blond hair knit in a tight, almost Japanese bun, her aura of seriousness and her Mediterranean luster outshone the blandly corn-fed and T-shirted students in whose midst she had materialized. Angela Verucci was not so much a girl, really: twenty-four years old, she'd already studied at Oxford before taking the Reeves Fellowship that had brought her to America. She spoke immaculate English, and though her accreditation was a mess, truly she was nearly as accomplished a medievalist as I was the day she appeared in my class. This was at Oregon State University, in Corvallis, where I'd been given a two-year postdoc after my six years at Irvine. Oregon State was the third stop in Angela Verucci's American tour—she'd also spent a year at Columbia and, as it happened, a term at Corcoran.

What does a single, thirty-year-old history professor do with the sweetest student he's ever had? He waits until the end of the semester, files a Circular of Intent with the Faculty Appropriateness Committee, and in early spring asks her to hike with him to the highest point in the county, a lookout over three mountain ranges called Sutter's Parlor. Angela Verucci arrived in heels, perhaps not completely grasping the sense of the invitation. We forsook the ascent in favor of a glass of Oregon Pinot Noir on a restaurant patio perched on the Willamette River—near enough, for the Brooklynite and the Sicilian, to an expedition.

We were married two years later, on the Italian island itself. The ceremony was deferentially Catholic; I didn't care. The wider circle of my acquaintances learned the happy details in a mass e-mail. Then Angela and I returned to our quiet rented bungalow in New Brunswick, New Jersey. I was at Rutgers then, on a second postdoc, and hungry for a tenure-track position. My job interviews were hardly unsuccessful: I was never summarily dismissed, instead always called back for second and third visits, always asked to teach a sample class. Afterward, polite notes flew back and forth, candidate and committee reassuring one another of how fine the experience had been, how glad we both were to have met. Only I never got a job.

So by the time I got the invitation to interview for a position at Corcoran, the New England pastures of my alma mater didn't appear such a poor fate. It was the week of Halloween, the weather glorious, so at the very least the day of the interview would be a nice jaunt. We left early, to roam a few New Hampshire back roads, then ate a picnic lunch beside Corcoran Pond before I checked in for an afternoon of meetings.

Corcoran looked implacable, though I knew it was changed. The school had been through financial shake-ups and tenure scandals; those had, in turn, purged most of the administrators and faculty I'd known. But the grounds, the crab apple trees and white clapboard, were eternal as a country-store calendar. While Angela took a memory tour, heading for her old dorm, I turned up for my scheduled tribunal. There, I was debriefed by peers, a couple of them younger than myself. The room was full of the usual tensions: some of these people had an investment in my candidacy, some had bets on other tables. No one was in the least sentimental about my status as alumnus—that was reserved, I supposed, for the dinner tonight, arranged in my honor at the president's house. After a finishing round of polite handclasps I was ferried to the president's office. On top of tonight's dinner, she'd also wanted to meet me alone. I figured it was a good sign.

The president asked how I'd liked the interview; we

made this and other small talk. She asked about my years at Corcoran, which I painted in rosy tones. Then she said: "Did you know Super Goat Man when you were a student here?"

"Sure," I said. "I mean, I never took a class with him."

"He surprised me by asking to join us at the dinner tonight—he usually doesn't bother with faculty socializing anymore."

"He's still here?" I was amazed Super Goat Man, of all people, had threaded his way through so many personnel shake-ups.

"Yes, though he's reduced to a kind of honorary presence. He doesn't actually teach now. I don't know if he'd be capable of it. But he's beloved. The students joke that he can be spotted strolling across Commons lawn twice a semester. And that if you want to get any time with him, you can join him on the stroll."

"He recognized my name?"

"He seemed to, yes. You should prepare yourself. He's quite infirm."

"How—how old is he?"

"Measured in years, I don't know. But there's been an accelerated aging process. You'll see."

Perhaps superheroism was a sort of toxin, like a steroid, one with a punitive cost to the body. I mused on this as I departed the president's office, crossed the Commons, and headed through the parking lot and downhill, to find the bench beside Corcoran Creek, a favorite spot, where Angela had said she'd wait. I saw my wife before she saw me, her feet tucked up on the slats, abandoned shoes beneath, her body curled around a big hardback biography of Rousseau. In the distance, dying October light drew long saddle-shaped curves on the White Mountains of New Hampshire. Suddenly I could picture us here for a long time, and picture it happily.

"How did it go?" she asked when she noticed me.

"Par: two friends, two enemies, one sleeper."

"And the president?"

"Nice, but she wasn't giving anything away." I put my hands on her shoulders. She closed the book.

"You seem distant," Angela said. "Memories?"

"Yes." In fact, I was thinking about Super Goat Man. I'd never before considered the sacrifice he'd made, enunciating his political views so long ago. Fruitlessly, it seemed to me. In exchanging his iconic, trapped-in-amber status, what had he gained? Had Super Goat Man really accomplished much outside the parameters of his comics? However unglamorous the chores, didn't kittens *need* rescuing from trees? Didn't Vest Man require periodic defeating? Why jettison Ralph Gersten if in the end all you attained was life as a campus mascot?

I wanted to convey some of this to Angela, but didn't know where to begin. "When you were here—" I began, then stopped.

"Yes?"

"Did you know Super Goat Man?"

I felt her stiffen. "Of course, everybody knew him," she said.

"He's still here." I watched her as I spoke. Her gaze dipped to the ground.

"You saw him?"

"No, but we will at dinner tonight."

"How . . . unexpected." Now Angela was the one in fugue.

"Did you study with him?"

"He rarely taught. I attended a few talks."

"I thought you didn't like that stuff."

She shrugged. "I was curious."

I waited to understand. Crickets had begun a chorus in the grass. The sun ebbed. Soon we'd need to visit our bed-and-breakfast outside campus, to change into fresh clothes for the dinner party. Ordinarily such gatherings were clumsy at best, with grudges incompletely smothered under the surface of the talk, among tenured faculty who knew one another far too well. Something in me now curdled at the prospect of this one. In fact, I'd begun to dread it.

"Everett." There was something Angela wanted to tell me.

I made a preemptive guess. "Did you have some sort of something with Super Goat Man?" This was how she and I blundered through one another's past liaisons—we'd never been systematic.

I moved around the bench, to try and look her in the eye.

"Just an—affair. Nothing."

"What's nothing?"

She shrugged, and flipped her fingers as though dispelling a small fog. "We fooled around a few times. It was stupid."

I felt the poison of bitterness leach into my bloodstream. "I don't know why but I find that totally disgusting."

"Oh, Everett." Angela raised her arms, moved to assuage me, knowing as she did my visceral possessiveness, the bolt of jealousy that shot through me when contemplating her real past, anytime it arose. Of course, she couldn't understand my special history with Super Goat Man. How could she if I didn't? I'd never even mentioned him.

"I was a silly girl." She spoke gently. "And I didn't know you yet."

Unsatisfied, I wished her to declare that the encounter had been abusive, an ethical violation. Not that I had any ground to stand on. Anyway, she was Italian in this, as in all things. It was just an affair.

"Do you want to skip the dinner?"

She scowled. "That's silly. He wouldn't even remember. And I don't care. It's really nothing, my darling. My love."

At the president's house Super Goat Man was the last to arrive, so I was allowed to fantasize briefly that I'd been spared. The sight, when he did come in, was startling. He'd not only aged, but shrunk—I doubted if he was even five feet tall. He was, as ever, barefooted, and wore white muslin pajamas, with purple piping. The knees of the pajama bottoms were smudged with mud. As he entered the room, creeping in among us as we stood with our cocktail glasses, I quickly saw the reason for the smudges: as Super Goat Man's rickety steps faltered he dropped briefly to all fours. There, on the ground, he'd shake himself, almost like a wet dog. Then he'd rise again, on palsied limbs.

No one took notice of this. The guests, the other faculty, were inured, polite. In this halting manner Super Goat Man made his way past us, to the dining room. Apparently he wasn't capable of mingling, or even necessarily of speech. He took a seat at the long table, his bunched face, his squinting eyes and wrinkled horns, nearly at the level of his place setting. So Super Goat Man's arrival curtailed cocktail hour, as we began drifting in behind him, almost guiltily. The president's husband showed us to our places, which had been carefully designated, though an accommodation was evidently being made for Super Goat Man, who'd plopped down where he liked and wasn't to be budged. I was at the right hand of the president, and the left of the chair of the hiring committee. Again, a good sign. Angela sat across from me, Super Goat Man many places away, at the other end of the table.

I actually managed to forget him for the duration of the meal. He was, so far as I could tell, silent at his feed, and the women on either side of him turned to their other partners, or conversed across the width of the table. Toward the end we were served a course of cognac and dessert, and the president's husband passed around cigars, which he bragged were Cuban. Some of the women fled their chairs to avoid the smoke; other guests rose and mingled again in the corners of the room. It was in this interval of disarrangement that Super Goat Man pushed himself off his chair and made his way to the seat at my left, which the president had vacated. He had to collapse to his knees only once on the way, and he offered no evidence of sacrificed dignity as he rose from the floor.

Angela remained in her seat. Unlike any of the American women, she'd accepted a cigar, and now leaned it into the flame of a lighter proffered by an older professor she'd been entertaining throughout the meal. Her eyes found mine as Super Goat Man approached. Her expression was curious, and not unsympathetic.

Super Goat Man prodded my arm with a finger. I turned and considered him. Black pupils gleamed behind a hedge of eyebrows. His resplendent tufts had thinned and spread—the hair of his face had been redistributed, to form a merciful gauze across his withered features.

"I . . . knew . . . your . . . father." His voice was mossy, sepulchral.

"Yes," I said simply, keeping my voice low. No one was paying us any attention, yet. Not apart from Angela.

"You . . . remember . . . ?"

"Of course."

"We . . . love . . . jazz . . ."

I wondered whether he meant my father or, somehow, me. I had in fact over the years come around to my father's love of jazz, though my preference was not so much Ornette Coleman and Rahsaan Roland Kirk as Duke Ellington and Fletcher Henderson.

"... poker ..."

"He cleaned you out," I reminded him.

"Yezz ... good times ... beautiful women ..." He struggled, swallowed hard, blinked. "All this controversy ... not worth it ..."

"My father was never involved in any controversy," I heard myself say, though I knew Super Goat Man was speaking only of himself, his lost career.

"No ... absolutely true ... knew how to live ..."

Angela had leaned back, pursing her lips to savor the cigar. I might have noticed the room's gabble of conversation had dampened somewhat—might have noticed it sooner, I mean.

"So ... many ... hangovers ..."

"But you and I have something in common besides my father," I told Super Goat Man.

"Yezz ... yezz ... ?"

"Of course we do," I began, and though I now understood we had the attention of the entire room, that the novelty of Super Goat Man's reminiscences had drawn every ear, I found myself unable to quit before I finished the thought. Further, having gained their attention, I allowed my voice to rise to a garrulous, plummy tone, as if I were starring in dinner theater. Before the line was half out of my mouth, I knew that the words, by airing the sort of laundry so desperately repressed in a community as precious as Corcoran, damned my candidacy. But that was a prize I no longer sought. Broader repercussions I could only guess at. My wife's eyes were on me now, her cigar's blunt tip flaring. I'd answer to her, later, if she gave me the chance.

It was the worst thing I could think to say. The impulse had formed in the grip of sexual jealousy, of course. But before it crossed my lips I knew my loathing had its origins in an even deeper place, the mind of a child wondering at his father's own susceptibility to the notion of a hero.

What I said was this: "I once saw you rescue a paper clip."

The
National Anthem

1/12/03

Dear M,

Our long letters are pleasing to me, but they do come slowly. Lulled by the intrinsic properties of e-mail, I've been willing to let most of my other correspondence slide down that slippery slope, into hectic witty ping-pong. But our deep connection, for twenty years or more now unrefreshed or diluted or whatever it would be by regular communications in person or on the phone, is precious to me, and demands more traditional letters, even if those mean long gaps. I suppose three-month breaks are not so much in a friendship once treated so casually that we let nearly a decade go by, eh?

You asked about A. We've finally broken it off, the end of a nearly three-year chapter in my life, and a secret chapter as well. For, apart from you, safely remote in Japan, I've confided in no one. Her horrible marriage survived us, a fact that would have seemed absurd to me at the beginning, if some time traveler had come back to whisper it in my ear. The break was mutual—mutual enough to give it that name—and I'd be helpless to guess who is the more scarred. We won't be friends, but we were never going to be. Dissolving a secret affair is eerily simple: A and I only had to quit lying that we didn't exist.

Did I tell you about "The National Anthem"? I don't think so. This was the first night we stole together from her husband, the first intentional rendezvous, at a bed-and-breakfast outside Portland, Maine. A always traveled with a Walkman and a wallet of CDs, and that night, as we lay entwined in a twee canopy bed, she insisted on playing me a song, though there was no way for us to listen to it together. Instead she cued it up and watched me while it played, her ungroggy eyes inspecting me from below the horizon of my chest, mine a posture of submission: James Carr singing "The Dark End of the Street." I recognized it, but I'd never listened closely before. It's a song of infidelity and hopeless love, full of doomed certainty that the lovers, the love, will fail.

"I've got a friend who calls that 'The National Anthem,' " she said.

I gave her what was surely a weak-sickly smile, though likely I thought it was a cool and dispassionate one, at the time. She didn't elaborate, just let it sink in. I didn't ask who the friend might be—the unspecificity seemed as essential to the mood between us as the dual rental cars, the welcoming basket of cookies and fruit we'd ignored downstairs, or the silent fucking we'd enjoyed, our orgasms discrete, in turn. To press one another back into the world of names, of our real individual lives, would have seemed a rent in the shroud of worldly arbitrariness which enclosed our passion. Of course this was morbid, I see it now.

"There's a Bob Dylan song," I said then. " 'Ninety Miles an Hour (Down a Dead End Street).' I think it's a cover, actually. Same thing: *We're on a bad motorcycle with a devil in the seat, going ninety miles an hour down a dead end street . . .*"

"Yes, but this is 'The National Anthem.' "

By refusing the comparison A put me on notice that this wasn't a dialogue, but a preemptive declaration. She'd be the one to manage our yearnings, by her foreknowledge of despair. Fair enough: her jadedness was what I'd been drawn to in the first place.

Of course you know, M, because I've told you stories, how we rode her jadedness—our bad motorcycle—down our own dead-end street. It wasn't kept anonymously cute, with baskets of cookies, for long. The perversity of the affair, it seems to me now, is that under cover of delivering her from the marriage she claimed to be so tired of, A and I climbed inside the armature of that marriage instead. By skulking at its foundations, its skirts, we only proved its superiority. However aggrieved she and R might be, however dubious their prospect, it wasn't a secret affair, wasn't nearly as contemptible as *us*. Certainly that can be the only explanation for why, in a world of motels and with my own apartment free, we so often met at her place—at theirs. And I think now that though I mimed indifference whenever she predicted imminent destruction, I'd *lusted* to destroy a marriage, that I was far more interested in R than I allowed myself to know.

But I don't want to make this letter about A. You've written at length about your uncertainties in your own marriage—written poignantly, then switched to a tone of flippancy, as though to reassure me not to be too concerned. Yet the flippancy is the most poignant of all—your joshing about your vagrant daily lusts in such an unguarded voice makes them real to me. Having never been to Japan, nor met your wife and child, I've been guilty of picturing it as some rosy, implacable surface, as though by moving from New York to Tokyo and entering a "traditional" Japanese marriage you'd migrated from the complicated world into an elegantly calm piece of eighteenth-century screen art. I'm probably not the first person guilty of finding it convenient to imagine my friends' lives are simpler than my own. It's also possible I began this letter by speaking of A in order to discredit myself as any sort of reasonable counsel, to put you in mind of my abhorrent track record (or maybe I'm just obsessed).

Let me be more honest. I don't spend all that much time imagining Japan. However much you and I speak of our contemporary lives, I picture you as I left you: eighteen years old. You and I were inseparable for the first three years at music and art, then distant in our senior year, then you vanished. Now you're a digital wraith. What would it take to displace the visceral daily knowledge of our teenage years—how extensive would the letters have to be? When I try to think of your marriage I instead tangle, helplessly, in the unexamined questions surrounding our first, lost friendship. I don't mean to suggest *anyone* doesn't find a muddle when they recall that year, launching from twelfth grade to the unknown. But it is usual to have you lucidly before me, daring me, by your good faith in these recent letters, to understand.

Do you remember my obsession with Bess Hersh? Do you remember how you played the go-between? That was junior year, just before the breach between us. Bess was a freshman, a ninth grader. You and I were giddy dorks in rapidly enlarging bodies, hoping that being two years older could stand in, with the younger girls, for the cool we'd never attained. I'll never forget the look on your face when you found me where I waited, at the little park beside the school, and said that Bess's appointed friend, her "second," had confirmed that she *liked me too.*

Bess Hersh saw through me shortly after that. I hadn't known what to do with this coup except bungle it when she and I had a moment alone, bungle it with my self-conscious tittering, my staring, my grin. I tried boy jokes on her, Steve Martin routines, and those don't work on girls in high school. What's required then is some stammering James Dean, with shy eyes cast to pavement. Those shy eyes are what give a girl as young as that breathing room, I think. You mastered those poses in short order—I'd wait until college.

Soon, agonizingly soon, Bess was on Sean Hyman's arm, and I felt that I'd only alerted the hipper Sean to her radiant presence among the new freshmen. But I still cling to that moment when I knew she'd mistaken me for cool, before I opened my mouth, while you were still ferrying messages between us so that she could project what she wished into the outline of me. I still picture her, too, as some sort of teenage sexual ideal, lost forever: her leggy slouching stride, the cinch of worn jeans over that impossible curve from her narrow waist to the scallop of her hips, her slightly too-big nose and fawny eyes. I wonder what kind of woman she grew into, whether I'd glance at her now. Once she gave me boners that nearly caused me to faint. Just typing her name is erotic to me still.

Funny, though, I don't remember speaking to her more than once or twice. I remember speaking with you about her, *chortling* about her, I should say, and scheming, and pining, and once, when we were safely alone in the Sheep's Meadow in Central Park, bellowing her name to the big empty sky. I recall talking this way with you too about Liz Kessel, Margaret Anodyne, and others. I recall the dopey, sexed-up love lyrics we'd write together, never to show to the girls. You and I were just clever enough, and schooled enough in *Mad* magazine, Woody Allen, Talking Heads, Frank Zappa, and Devo, to ironize our sprung lusts, to find the chaos of our new-yearning hearts bitterly funny.

When, six months on, you first began combing your hair differently, and when you began listening to New Romantic bands, and when you began dating Tu-Lin, I was disenchanted with you, M. Violently disenchanted, it seems to me now. I felt all the music you listened to was wrong, a betrayal—you'd quit liking the inane clever stuff, and moved on to music that felt postured and sexy instead. I felt you'd forgotten yourself, and I tried to show you what you'd forgotten. When I'd third around with you and your new Vietnamese girlfriend, I'd seek to remind you of our secret languages, our jokes—if they hadn't worked on Bess they should at least still mean something to you—but those japes now fell flat, and you'd rebuff me, embarrassed.

Of course the worse I fared the harder I tried. For a while. Then that became our falling-out. I must have appeared so angry—this is painful speculation, now. Of course, what seemed so elaborately *cultural* or *aesthetic* to me at the time—I faulted you for hairstyle, music, Tu-Lin's Asianness—all appears simply emotional in retrospect. I was threatened by the fact that you'd gone from pining for girls to having them, sure. But I'd also invested in you all my intimations of what I was about to surrender in myself, by growing up. By investing them in you I could make them something to loathe, rather than fear. Loathing was safer.

Oh, the simple pain of growing up at different speeds!

A page or two ago I supposed I was going to build back from this reminiscence, to some musings on your current quandary, your adult ambivalence about the commitments you entered when you married (I nearly wrote *entered precociously*, but that's only the case by my retarded standard). But I find I'm reeling even deeper into the past. When I was seven or eight, years before you and I had met, my parents befriended a young couple, weirdly named August and Sincerely. I guess those were their hippie names— at least Sincerely's must have been. August was a war resister. My parents had sort of adopted him during his trial, for he'd made the gesture of throwing himself an eighteenth birthday party in the office of his local draft board, a dippy bit of agitprop which got him singled out, two years later, for prosecution. Sincerely was a potter, with a muddy wheel and a red-brick kiln in the backyard of her apartment. She was blond and stolid and unpretentious, the kind of woman who'd impress me now as mannish, a lesbian perhaps, at least as a more plausible candidate for chumming around than for an attraction (I felt she was a woman, then, but she must have been barely twenty, if that).

We'd visit Sincerely often during the six or eight months while August served out his sentence, sit in the yard sipping iced tea she'd poured with clay-stained hands, and in that time I very simply—and articulately, to myself—fell in love. I was still pre-sexual enough to isolate my feelings for Sincerely as romantic and pure. In stories like this one children are supposed to get mixed up, and to imagine that adults will stop and wait for them to grow up, but I wasn't confused for a moment. I understood that my love for Sincerely pertained to the idea of what kind of woman I meant to love in my future life as a man. I promised myself she would be exactly like Sincerely, and that when I met her I would love her perfectly and resolutely, that I would be better to her than I have in fact ever been to anyone—than anyone's ever been to anyone else.

So my love wasn't damaged by August's return from jail (he'd never gone upstate, instead served his whole time in the Brooklyn House of Detention, on Atlantic Avenue). I didn't even bother to resent his possession of Sincerely, which I saw as intrinsically flawed by grown-up sex and diffidence. August wasn't a worthy rival, and so I just went on secretly loving Sincerely with my childish idealism. The moron-genius of my young self felt it knew better than any adult how to love, felt certain it wouldn't blow the chance if it were given one. Not one day I've lived since has satisfied that standard. Of course, it is strange and sad for me now to see a shade of future triangulation in that emotional arrangement—I'd cast August as an early stand-in for R, a man I would pretend was irrelevant even as I fitted myself into his place in life.

What I'd promised to hold on to then, M, is the same thing I'd raged against losing when you began to grow away from me, when I failed the test presented by your sultry new self that senior year. How ashamed that promiser would be to learn—had some malicious time traveler drifted back to whisper it in his ear—about the pointless ruin of my years with A. Those promises we make to ourselves when we are younger, about how we mean to conduct our adult lives, can it be true we break every last one of them? All except for one, I suppose: the promise to judge ourselves by those standards, the promise to remember the child who would be so appalled by compromise, the child who would find jadedness wicked.

Yes, my childish self would read this letter and think me poisoned with knowledge, but the truth is that what I flung against A so recklessly *was* my innocence, preserved in a useless form. The revving heart of my hopefulness, kicked into gear anew, is the most precious thing about me, I refuse to vilify it. I hope I fall in love again. But it's a crude innocence that fails to make the distinctions that might have protected me from A, and A from me. For by imagining I could save her from her marriage, by that blustery optimism by which I concealed from myself my own despair at the cul-de-sac lust had led us into, I forced her to compensate by playing the jaded one on both our behalves. What I mean to say is that I forced her to play me that song, M, by grinning at her like a loon. Like the way I grinned at Bess Hersh. I gave A no choice but to be the dark lady, by being the moron-child who thought love could repair what love had wrecked. A motorcycle that's gone off a cliff isn't repaired by another motorcycle.

Well, I've failed. This whole letter is about A, I see that now. You wonder whether you can stand never to know the touch of a fresh hand, the trembling flavor of a new kiss, and I'm desperately trying to keep from telling you the little I know: it's sweeter than anything, for a moment. For just a moment, there's nothing else. As to all you're weighing it against, your wife and child, I know less than nothing. The wisdom of your ambivalence, the whimsical, faux-jaded wit you share in your letter, as you contemplate the beauties around you, all that poise will be shattered if you act— I can promise you that much. You're more innocent than you know. I speak to you from the dark end of the street, but it's a less informed place than you'd think. All I can do for you is frame the question I've framed for myself: Where to steer the speeding motorcycle of one's own innocence? How to make it a gift instead of a curse?

I think we need a new national anthem.

I'm ending this letter without saying anything about your incredible tale of the salaryman masturbating on the subway. Well, there, I've mentioned it. I'm also grateful to know that Godzilla's not what he's cracked up to be, that he's just another mediocre slugger with a good agent and a memorable nickname. What a joy it would be to see the Yankees really take a pratfall on that move. Bad enough when they pillage the other American teams, but that the world is their oyster too has become unbearable. Of course, the Mets go on signing haggard veterans and I think there's no hope at all, but you can be certain

Giuseppe and I will be out at Shea having our hearts broken this May, as always. In our hearts it's always spring, or 1969, or something like that. I only wish we had some outfielders who could catch the ball.

Yours,

E